LOVE AT FIRST FIGHT

CARRIE AARONS

Copyright © 2020 by Carrie Aarons

All rights reserved.

No part of this book may be reproduced in any form or by any electronic or mechanical means, including information storage and retrieval systems, without written permission from the author, except for the use of brief quotations in a book review.

This is a work of fiction. Names, characters, businesses, places, events and incidents are either the products of the author's imagination or used in a fictitious manner. Any resemblance to actual persons, living or dead, or actual events is purely coincidental.

Editing done by Proofing Style.

Cover designed by Okay Creations.

Do you want your **FREE** Carrie Aarons eBook?

All you have to do is **sign up for my newsletter**, and you'll immediately receive your free book!

For my daughter, with whom I was stuck in quarantine with during the penning of this story.
Everything I do is for you, even if it means writing late into the night or when you're taking naps. Or when you're pulling at my hand to let you give me a "checkup" for the sixtieth time that day.
I love you more than I could ever put into words.

1

MOLLY

The universe is seriously trying to conspire against me.

I swear it, whoever is sitting up there in the clouds accidentally poured salt in their coffee this morning, or for the past months' worth of mornings, and is taking it out on me.

I'm standing in the aisle of the Jitney, staring down at my threadbare, three-year-old suitcase that just popped a spring and busted open in front of everyone. And when I say everyone, I mean the hippest millennials able to rent a summer house in the Hamptons, to New York's elite that think it's cute to still take the bus to their million-dollar vacation abodes.

My baby pink cotton underwear is on the armrest of a forty-something blond woman's seat. My toothbrush lays in the middle of the bus, bristles now unusable. I'm pretty sure I heard my perfume crack, and I'm positive it's leaking all over the dozen items still trapped within the faulty travel case. Half my shirts are littered in front of me, while my string bikinis dangle perilously in between the teeth on the zipper of the bag.

I *pray* that the vibrator I packed and then unpacked and

then packed a dozen times had enough sense to stay in this broken bag.

"Do you need help?" someone behind me says, but they sound annoyed.

I'm holding up the entire line of people trying to board this bus, and now I'm sure everyone is ticked at me for the extra five minutes I've made them wait before they can get to weekend paradise. Don't mess with New Yorkers work-week escape from the city, it won't end well.

Bending, I begin to shove all of my things back into the tattered suitcase while also trying to hold it shut and keep anything else from falling out. My face heats every time someone watches me snatch a pair of underwear or a bra, and no one already seated offers to help.

The thing is, I shouldn't even be on this bus. I should be riding shotgun in my boyfriend's car, on the way to the house share we went in on with his friends. In the months leading up to June twenty-fifth, all I thought about was the salty ocean breeze whipping through my hair as Justin drove us down a coastal highway. I thought about days on the beach and nights of romantic dinners and sitting on a deck overlooking the sea. I thought about getting closer as a couple, falling more in love, and forming a tighter bond with his friends, who we'd be sharing a house with.

Now all I'm thinking about is how embarrassed I am to be cleaning up my unmentionables in front of total strangers. Well, that and how heartbroken I am.

My boyfriend, now ex-boyfriend, of exactly one year and a month decided to take a job in Singapore—and not ask me to go with him. Not only did he not ask me to go with him, but he made no indication of the move. Not when he was tying up loose ends like the lease on his West Village apartment. Not when he gave notice at his current job and I kept calling his secretary to connect me to Justin during the day. Not even when he packed up most of his things five days before the move and shipped them overseas.

No, my stellar pick for the man I'd decided to fall in love with told me he was moving *an hour* before his plane took off, via text, and proceeded to dump me in the most asshole of fashions.

You've never been blindsided until you're at work, in your blissful bubble of being in love, having a great job and thinking you've figured it all out, and your boyfriend texts you that he's about to take off for his new life in Singapore. That while he's loved the time you've shared, he is looking forward to this adventure without attachments. And then disconnects his number!

Nope, this is definitely not the place I should be. I wavered on whether I'd even come out to the Hamptons, because five of the other six people in the house are Justin's friends. We were supposed to make six and seven, and then my best friend, Heather, made eight. Now it's just Heather and me, with five of Justin's closest pals, and I'm quaking in my heartbroken boots.

I know they'll be supportive, as they're all pissed he left without giving them notice as well. And I have the bulk of my money invested into this summer house, no matter if my ex-boyfriend helped me out with part of my share.

But it was Heather who coaxed me from my sulking shell and told me to chin up because he wasn't coming back. I could either spend the summer eating takeout Chinese in my fifth-floor walk-up, or I could spend it sunning on some of the most classy beaches on the East Coast. When she put it that way, I knew I'd swallow my pride to at least get a tan.

After cramming my suitcase shut and scurrying off to a seat, I huff out a breath when the whole saga is over.

The rest of the bus ride is uneventful, a three-hour journey that I spend most of with my eyes closed and head resting against the bus window. When we finally get to the drop off point, I have to clutch my suitcase with two arms the entire way down the steps of the Jitney to keep it from springing open.

Thank God I thought ahead and ordered an Uber, because the thought of standing at this bus stop waiting for a taxi makes my already rising temper flare. And I'm not much of a hothead. It's just been a trying month.

My junky bag gets thrown in the trunk, and then I fold myself into a neon green Chevy that's bumping Bob Marley. "Everything's Gonna Be Alright" sings to me through the radio, and I think maybe I'll take this as a sign. Maybe the universe has gotten over the bone it had to pick with me.

The Uber comes to a stop at a red light, and the hum of a motorcycle engine coming up on the right of the car deafens me. I didn't even realize the residents of the Hamptons put up with motorcycles; I thought they'd be too noisy for the stuffy old geezers. And yes, I have a bone to pick with this beach town. Being a girl from a working-class New Jersey family, who spent summers in a tiny rental of the ever classy Seaside, New Jersey, I always viewed this as the place for people who stuck their noses up at people like my parents.

I only agreed to summer here because Justin wanted to, and I would have done anything to please him. I could barely scrape together the money to buy into the shared pot of this rental, but I'd eaten crackers for basically the month of March so I could afford it. Even then, Justin had covered a bulk of my financial portion. Before he left for Singapore, he hadn't asked for that back or pulled his money, so I guess I could thank him for that generous parting gift.

My vision slides over as the motorcycle pulls up alongside the Chevy I sit in, and the moment the driver's eyes glance at my tinted window, my stomach plummets through the floor of the car.

I pray to all that is holy that this tint is thick enough that those midnight blue eyes, the color of inky purple lust, can't see me. Screw you, universe, because apparently that song was not a peace offering but a trick to throw me off your evil scent.

You see, no good stroke of luck would have Smith Redfield be the first familiar person I lay eyes on when I stepped foot in the Hamptons.

Because the only thing worse than spending the summer without the boyfriend who just dumped you and literally took off for another country, is spending it with his sex-on-a-stick best friend.

Who also happens to hate every single one of your guts.

2

SMITH

The Chevy next to me, the color of one of those highlighters that exploded on me in elementary school, is playing Bob Marley so loudly that I can hear it over the thrum of my engine.

I chuckle, thinking of how out of place it seems in the middle of downtown Sag Harbor, but have to give props to the driver. Being on a motorcycle gives me a rare glimpse into the car activities of many, but not this guy. His windows are so tinted that I can barely see through the windshield, which is illegal.

Not that I'd ever report anyone for that kind of shit. *Do you, man*, I think before the light turns green and I'm off to the races.

The whip of the salty ocean air in my face might be one of my favorite sensations ever. I might be considered too badass for these parts, but I'm also a businessman, which means I can rub elbows if I choose to. Or most times, if it serves me a purpose.

See, I don't do things I don't want to, unless they result in the end goal of earning me something I *do* want. And when it comes to this summer, well, it's a little bit of both.

I want to be here, because where better to party and let off steam from my life in the city than Manhattan's favorite beach town? But I also don't want to be here, in light of recent events.

I curse my best friend, Justin, for coordinating the rental of a summer share house and then taking off to start a new life in Singapore. Not only am I pissed that he took off without much notice, because what kind of childhood buddy does that? But it's caused a shitload of complications for me. I've had to take over communications with the rental company, and the agents haven't taken kindly to that. Because the agents on this island are stuck up and pretentious. They expect things to go a certain way, or maybe just to sit in their cushy offices and not work at all because people in the Hamptons "don't make waves."

How ironic for a beach town.

Either way, I'm ticked off just pulling up to the massive waterfront mansion. Justin and I have been best buds since we were eleven, and I'm not typically the guy to get hurt and upset by another dude's actions, but I would never take off like he did. It's like he doesn't give a shit about anyone or anything he left behind, and even my issues-with-commitment ass can't relate to that.

Parking my bike and hopping off, I cut the engine and stare at the enormous Hamptons-shingled house in front of me. With six bedrooms, a pool table, hot tub, in-ground swimming pool, tennis court, and full chef's kitchen—it's obnoxious. The eight thirty-somethings who are about to occupy this place for two full months are not going to use half of it, and most of us will probably sleep until one p.m. after haunting the local hot spots until all hours of the morning.

Well, not *all* of us. The house is made up of two couples, Jacinda and Peter, and Ray and Marta. Followed by a girl named Heather who I've met twice or so, then there is me.

Last but not least, *she's* still coming to stay the summer. It boils my blood just thinking about that cornsilk hair glinting every day in the sunlight.

Shaking my head to knock her out of it, I focus on the task at hand. There are about seventy boxes piled high in front of the door. I'm sure those are the groceries and supplies Jacinda said she'd ordered ahead so no one would have to go to the store after the two-hour drive from the city. But of course, I got here first, and will have to lug them all inside.

As if I didn't do enough manual labor at the new restaurant location today. Another reason I didn't want to spend my summer in the Hamptons? I'm opening a third restaurant with my business partner, Campbell. We have two highly successful Italian places, one in midtown Manhattan and the other on the Upper West Side, and he finally convinced me to open up a third. They're not a chain or fast casual, they're respectable eateries with James Beard Award-caliber chefs.

It's my absolute passion, one I fell into as an eighteen-year-old kid who didn't want to go to college. My father had shoved me out the door and told me to get to work then. I somehow ended up as a dishwasher in one of the most notable French kitchens in the city, and from that point forward, fell in love with the whole industry. The grind of it, the hard work equaling up to a finished product. I began to rub elbows with some of the most influential chefs and restaurant owners in the world, and by the time I turned twenty-five, was managing a Michelin star steakhouse. Two years later, Campbell approached me about opening our own place, and my dream was born.

But balancing my vacation plans with my workaholic tendencies won't be easy this summer. Whenever we open a place, do a renovation, or even rework a sitting plan at one of our restaurants, I want to be involved on the ground level. But with everything that's happened in the last six months, Campbell has warned me that I better take a step back for my own mental health. The break has been nice, but I'm getting to the point of grief boredom, and I need an outlet.

I'm about to head to the front porch and tackle the boxes when the sound of wheels on pavement has me turning my head.

The green Chevy, the one I was stopped next to at the light, pulls down the driveway. And now I'm thoroughly confused. What the heck is Bob Marley doing here?

The back passenger side door opens, and the main reason I'm furious with Justin steps out.

Molly Archer.

Justin's petite, blonde, fairylike ex-girlfriend.

City school teacher for the underprivileged.

Sally homemaker who prefers baking blueberry muffins on a Saturday night than tipping back vodka shots.

The fair-skinned, doe-eyed woman who looks like a Swedish princess and gets my cock harder than any of the busty brunettes I woo on the island of Manhattan.

I fucking hate that she affects me in any way, but loathe even more that she's the seventh guest in our summer house. And I don't even have the buffer of Justin between us anymore. It's a miracle I didn't revoke her stay, but I wasn't going to cover her share. Over my dead body was I going to replace Mother Teresa's money, even if it meant I could throw her out of the rental.

Her eyes drop to the ground as soon as she sees me standing in front of the house, but then she regains that bright, infuriating smile.

"Hey, Smith, good to see you. How was your drive?" Her voice is full of fake sunshine.

Why does it piss me off even more that no matter how mean I am to this woman, she always attempts to be cordial? Sometimes I see just how far I can push her until she snaps.

"It was better than yours." I sneer, tossing my head in the

direction of the retreating Uber. "You couldn't afford to take an Uber all the way from the city. Let me guess, did you take the train?"

The way I phrase it, it definitely sounds as if I'm making it known the train is for peasants.

Her hair blows in the breeze as some of the friendliness dies in her swirling hazel eyes. "No, I took the Jitney."

"Even more pathetic." I snort, turning my back on her.

I don't mean to be such a dick, I swear I don't. But over the last year, I've had to put up some kind of shield. I've had to demonize her in my head, make it like she's the worst kind of person. I've had to lie to my own brain to trick it into thinking that Molly Archer is a stuck-up brat.

Because if I don't, I'll have to admit she's my kryptonite.

I'll have to admit that the minute Justin introduced her to me a year ago, I understood. It clicked.

I know what it feels like to fall in love at first sight. Because I did, with her.

And then she went on to fall in love with my best friend.

3

MOLLY

The house is even more gorgeous than the pictures Justin had shown me.

An all-white shingled outside, like those fancy Kennedy houses on the Cape of Massachusetts, with columns up the front leading to an austere balcony wrapping around the second floor of the house. The gardens are filled with fragrant flowers, hydrangeas, and peonies. The lawn is expertly manicured, and you can hear the lap of the ocean waves even from the driveway.

The interior is even more stunning. Done in floral and striped blue and white, whoever decorated this place must have spent a pretty penny. It's easily the most beautiful home I've ever stepped foot in, much less spent a day in. My stomach does a giddy backflip thinking about the fact that I get to spend the entire summer here.

With each new room I walk into, my jaw drops even farther. Beautiful hardwood floors, gleaming wood craftsmanship on the walls, glass vases and plush throw pillows on antique couches. Marble countertops, smooth pure white cabinets, king-sized beds with sheets that look like they cost more than my monthly rent. Every window overlooks the majestic Atlantic Ocean, that is, if your eyes don't focus on the gorgeous swimming pool and hot tub conveniently located in the backyard.

The place is a palace, and as Smith Redfield just pointed out, I'm a peasant.

Why did he have to be standing on the driveway the moment I arrived? I was probably red-faced and sweating from lugging my broken suitcase around, and I hadn't bothered to change out of my camp counselor clothes before boarding the Jitney. There is no doubt I look like some kind of baby bunny in an olive green polo, when he's used to big-boobed, long-legged supermodels.

And my gosh, did he have to be that drop-dead gorgeous? Having looks like that isn't even fair, by any standards. Smith is statuesque, at least a foot or more taller than my short five three. With long, muscular legs and a tapered waist leading up to broad pecs and shoulders, he's built like the perfect specimen of a man. He's hit that sweet spot with his physique, not body builder gross with his muscles, but just chiseled enough that it's effortless sexy. And then there is his coloring, and his face. My God, his skin is that perfect Italian shade of olive, and I just know that it'll tan in the sun this summer, making him even more irresistible. With a chiseled jaw, blue eyes that twinkle more than sapphire, and a mouth that seems to remain in a permanent devious smirk, Smith is ... *hot*. I'm pretty sure if you looked up the definition of the word in the dictionary, his picture would be there.

Of course, I shouldn't be thinking about him in this way. Not only because he hates me with the heat of a thousand suns, but because he is my ex-boyfriend's best friend. It's weird for me to ogle Justin's closest childhood friend. And it's not as if he'd *ever* look at me the same way. I've seen the girls he dates, and they're so far from me it's laughable.

"Why the hell would you put those there?" He lobs an insult my way as my hand freezes mid-air.

In it is a box of cereal, one I was about to place next to the four others that Jacinda had ordered with the groceries.

"I thought this would be a good spot. It's in the pantry, but clear and in the line of sight because most people will reach for it in the morning ..." I hate that my voice sounds unsure.

"Clearly you've never lived in a summer house." He blows out an annoyed breath.

Seriously? He's getting pissy over corn flakes? Is there nothing I can do right with this guy?

"No, I haven't. If there is a system you usually put in place, please let me know." I try to paste on a friendly face.

All he does is grimace at me. "You really don't have to help in here, I got it."

"I want to carry my weight around here, and I really don't mind. I love to cook, so it'll be good to familiarize myself with the kitchen."

Smith's back is to me as he places wineglasses onto a shelf, but I hear him mutter. "Yeah, since you won't be carrying it financially."

"What was that?" I snap, because I'll put up with petty comments, not downright rude ones.

His T-shirt rides up, revealing a strip of smooth, olive back muscle, and I have to retain the anger that just flooded my body.

"I just know that Justin kept his money in the house, guess that's a pretty good deal for you." There is so much taunting and contempt in his voice.

My face burns with shame, and I wish so badly I could punch Smith and do some damage. If there is one thing I won't tolerate, it's someone being nasty about my career.

"Not all of us can make millions, but I love my job. I'm making a difference, and what's more, I love watching my students succeed and believe in themselves. If that isn't the type of thing that impresses you simply because I don't make six or seven figures, then I'm perfectly fine with that. Believe me, I don't need your approval as much as your overinflated ego might think, Smith."

I must have smacked him with a two-by-four of knowledge he wasn't expecting, because the look on his face when he turns around is a mix of shock, and possibly something like admiration.

"Hello?" I hear the front door open, and my best friend's voice travels down the hall.

Oh thank God, saved by Heather. I take that as my chance to escape my scowling tall, dark and handsome enemy in the kitchen, and book it to the foyer.

"You're here!" I cheer, throwing my arms around her.

She chuckles. "Are we ready to get this summer started off right?"

Backing up, she pulls an arm out from behind her back and pulls out a bottle of champagne. I clap like it's Christmas morning. Then she pulls her other arm out and there is a bottle of orange juice.

"You read my mind." I smirk. "Not only could I use some vitamin D, but you just saved me from a hatefest in the kitchen."

Heather peers around me. "Oh, is Smith here?"

"It's been just us for the past hour, and needless to say, it's been sufficiently hostile." I can feel the worry lines forming on my forehead already.

She rolls her eyes. "I have no idea what Mr. Perfect has to be so pissed off about. He's rich, hot as sin, and got that whole bad boy thing going on."

A flash of guilt hits me square in the gut. "Heath, you know he hasn't had it easy the past couple of months."

My heart openly aches for him, even if he's been nothing but a jerk since we stepped foot in the house.

"The guy was a shithead to you even before Stephanie passed, so that's not the excuse. Whatever, he better behave himself this summer. And if not, we'll ignore him. This is our summer of freedom, of taking back our self-worth!"

She pumps her fist in the air like she's the cheerleader of this summer vacation and I should get on board with the pep squad. I have to admit, I'm so glad I decided to invite her when Justin said we needed an eighth person for the house. If I had still been in a relationship, it still would have been awesome to spend the summer with my best friend. We barely get to see each other in between work in the city these days, and I was looking forward to some girl time.

But now that I got dumped and was in a house consisting mainly of my ex's crew, I am thanking my lucky stars that I decided to include her. I would never be able to survive the summer without her and am still doubting I'll get through it in one piece. My head and my heart both feel like they're being pulled in seventeen different directions, and I'm hoping that with some relaxation and lots of days spent on the sand, I'll start to feel whole again.

"All right, let's go pour some drinks. I could sure use one, and I know you definitely could use one." She passes me, expecting me to follow her.

I do, breathing easier just having her in the house.

Plan for the summer? Spend as much time as possible cocktailing with Heather, and avoid Smith at all costs.

4

SMITH

"Who's ready for margaritas?" Peter booms as he walks in the door, his personality larger than life.

I was in one of the three sitting rooms in the house, texting Campbell about some work on the bar area in the new restaurant, when my other best friend walks in the door. Shortly after I hear him, I see him walk into the room I'm in, carrying a massive frozen margarita machine.

"Cinda, you let him buy that?" I chuckle, surprised that his girlfriend let him spring for the thing he'd been talking about for months.

Not that he couldn't afford it on his doctor's salary, but she kept saying it was tacky.

Jacinda walks into the room, all gorgeous swathing skirts and Mother Earth energy, and rolls her eyes. "I admitted I'd like a strawberry daiquiri this summer, and next thing I knew he was one-clicking it on Amazon."

"This place is incredible, man. Props to Justin, though he'll be missing it." Peter shrugs, his NYU T-shirt showing off his alma matter.

The three of us, Justin, Peter and I, grew up on the same

street in Queens. We played street hockey until the streetlights came on, were the little shitheads toilet-papering people's houses on mischief night, and started competing for the attention of girls the day we turned thirteen.

Justin was the most well-off of us all, which made him the stuck-up, cocky, financial guy of the group. He was the showboat, always self-assured and somewhat narcissistic. But the guy was the first one to come to your aid in a crisis, and for that I'd always be grateful. I was the quieter of us three, the loner in the group of best friends. I had the more creative brain, and never followed a traditional path.

Then there's Peter, who became a doctor. I'm not surprised in the least, since he was the math and science club kid out of our group. He's now one of the most successful orthopedists in midtown Manhattan and met his match in Jacinda four years ago. She's the "mom" of our group, always organizing activities, cleaning up after us, and bossing us around. I love her like she's family now, and soon she will be. I know Peter has an engagement ring in his suitcase that he's planning to give her this summer.

"Anyone home?" Marta's voice comes from the front door.

"In here, boo!" Jacinda calls from the living room.

Peter lopes off to unload the margarita machine into the kitchen, and Marta comes bounding into the room, hugging Jacinda's neck. Her boyfriend, Ray, follows, smiling easily at me in greeting.

Marta and Ray kind of fell into the group naturally. Marta grew up with the three of us as well, but was best friends with my twin sister, Stephanie. When she ...

I can't even force myself to think the words, so I glaze over them in my brain. A couple years ago, Marta hung out with us guys more, and formed a friendship with Jacinda. Now, they were inseparable, and it just made sense once Marta met Ray two years ago that they'd mold into our crew.

Ray is nice enough, though he is about eight years older than the rest of us. He's a doctor, too, a hand surgeon, so he and Peter get along. The guy is chill, much to my appreciation, and he is good to Marta, which is all I could ask for.

My twin sister's best friend and I have a close relationship, almost as if she was another one of the Redfield brood, but we'd coped differently in the past six months. Marta wanted to talk about Stephanie all the time, remember her fondly, and I just couldn't.

"How long have you been here?" Marta asks, bending to where I sit on the couch and kissing my cheek.

"About two, two and a half hours. Unloaded the shit ton of groceries Cinda bought. Thanks for that." I send Jacinda a snarky smile.

She pats my cheek like I'm a lap dog. "You're welcome. I'll make you a Tom Collins in return."

"That sounds great. Considering you guys left me alone with *her*." I jerk a thumb to the stairs, and they immediately know who I'm talking about.

"Oh, is she here?" Jacinda whispers as if we're about to have an epic gossip session.

"Yes. Arrived on the Jitney." I say the last word as if it's scum between my toes.

Marta rolls her eyes. "The Jitney is convenient and I recall you taking it the first year we came out here."

I wave her off as if this never happened. "Whatever. Her little friend is here, too."

Jacinda looks torn. "This is going to be epically awkward without Justin here. I just feel so bad for her. Please try to be nice. She's a sweet girl."

Peter calls to her from the kitchen, and she walks out of the room.

Marta turns to Ray. "Babe, can you get the bags out of the car?"

He nods, kisses her cheek, and then goes to do her bidding. They're a perfect match, these two.

But then she rounds on me, a finger in my face. "Listen to me right now. I will not sit by this entire summer while you bully that girl and pretend like you're not head over heels in love with her. She and Justin are done, and I'm kind of glad that asshat is halfway around the world. Now is your time to tell her how you feel. I'll literally punch you in the balls if August comes around and you're still sulking in your Tom Collins every night. Got it?"

Leave it to my surrogate sister to set me straight. Marta is the only one who knows my true feelings about Molly, mostly because Stephanie suspected it the first month she and Justin got together. Ever since December, Marta has been on my back to tell Molly how I really feel. By using the excuse that life is too short.

As if I don't know that from firsthand shit experience.

"Don't push me on this," I warn, ice in my voice.

She looks at me like I'm the most pathetic thing she's ever seen and then stalks off.

I can't explain the feeling that came over me the first time I laid eyes on Molly. It wasn't a bolt of lightning; the room didn't fade into tones of pink and red. There were no bells chiming in my ears.

No, it was a slow, fuzzy feeling that took over my brain, my heart. It was if my whole being just said, "Ah, there she is. I found her," and it all just clicked into place. She hadn't said one word to me, and beyond a shadow of a doubt, I knew this was the woman I was meant to spend the rest of my life with.

It's completely unbelievable, whenever you hear someone

tell a story like that. You think they're fucking lying about how they met their spouse, or when they knew that person was the one. For years, I've been rolling my eyes or gagging in my mouth when a sorry-ass guy waxed poetic like that. Shit like that doesn't happen, and I've never been one to think I'd ever settle down or get married. It never seemed like something I'd enjoy, and I had enough family surrounding me for years.

With my brood of seven brothers and sisters, dozens of aunts and uncles, and a gaggle of cousins that could easily fill a movie theater, I had plenty of love and chaos around me growing up. I've seen arguments, cheating, marital drama, and everything of the sort. No thanks, it didn't interest me in the least.

Until I met her. The night Justin brought her to Jacinda and Peter's apartment, I started planning the rest of my life. With her. I saw it all so clearly, and then was smacked back down to earth the minute he groped her ass and kissed her up against the marble island as if no one was watching. She broke it off and giggled, embarrassed, and I could tell she was in so deep with him after just a month of seeing each other.

I'd never betray my best friend, and the girl I'd only just said hello to for the first time was clearly infatuated with him. Obviously, the epiphany I had looking at her had not happened on her end, and that made me burn with rage even more.

So I slotted her in the villain role. I've been a total douche each time I see her, making it a point to pick on her like we were on the kindergarten playground.

And perfect little Molly, she just stood there and took it while I crushed her soul. Never lashed out, or fought back. She just pastes on a smile with each new interaction, and I could tell she was hoping I'd come around.

Now she's living in my rental house for the entire summer, single as a lone wolf, and I can already feel my defenses starting to slip.

But I have to keep them up, remember why she can never be mine. Not only has my best friend been there, but now, I'm in no place to love someone the way she deserves to be loved.

I'm damaged goods, and there is no way I'm letting her touch my issues with a ten-foot pole.

5

MOLLY

Turning to examine myself in the mirror, I shake my head defiantly.

"Absolutely not."

I begin to untie the straps of the white halter eyelet dress Heather selected for me, and she captures my hands in hers.

"No, no, you *have* to! It looks *incredible*. Trust me, this is the precedent you want to set tonight as we move into your single summer."

I turn back to the mirror, skeptical, and two seconds away from taking it off. The scrap of material is way too short, even on my five-three frame. It's flirty and stands out, as white will typically do in a crowd. The halter style top accentuates what little amount of cleavage I have, and I just feel way too exposed in it.

"I can't, Heather. I don't feel comfortable." I shrug a shoulder.

She's provided me with a smoky eye and even took my hair off my shoulders in a sleek chignon. I got the full Heather Blinc makeover, and I have to admit ... I look good.

"Comfortable is so not the vibe we're going for. We're going independent, 'hear me roar' sex kitten. You're a fucking catch, and I won't have you doubting that anymore. You had a month, now it's time to get back out on the market. Have a few one-night stands, dance with some randoms, make this summer your bitch!"

I have to chuckle, because she's so ridiculous. "Yeah, totally sounds like me."

Heather flips her long, auburn hair over her shoulder. I've envied that hair since we were in sixth grade, when she told Tammy Canoots to eat shit on the playground after she pushed me down a slide. It was the moment we became best friends, and I've been jealously eyeing her hair since. Where mine is still nice, it holds no curl. My thick, straight blond hair can do little more than wave in the worst of humidity. Whereas Heather's looks like some kind of Pantene commercial where every girl has impossibly shiny, curled locks down to their butt.

With her gorgeous hair and baby pink slip dress, she looks like she belongs in some London nightclub VIP booth, rather than a beachside bar in the Hamptons. But no matter where she goes, or dresses, Heather typically seems to fit in. She's a social butterfly, one whose job at a fashion magazine gives her access to the best trends and newest products. She can charm a venomous snake, and I get the feeling she might try to do just that with Smith this summer.

The only thing stopping her is my bitter annoyance toward his hatred of me.

"Come on, it's time for shots!" She claps her hands, and I cringe.

"Do we have to?"

"Just one for courage, bottoms up!" The glass she hands me smells suspiciously like tequila.

I don't protest again, because honestly, I need it if I'm going out in this dress. The liquid burns, but gives me the dose of courage I think I need.

When we make it down the stairs, Jacinda, Peter, and Smith are all waiting by the front door.

"Marta and Ray aren't coming, so it looks like the five of us." Jacinda smiles at me. "I'm glad we'll get some more time together this summer."

Is she? It always struck me that she was more into being Justin's friend than wanting to include me in their circle, but I'll have to take her word on it.

"Me too."

"I called us a cab, I think it just pulled up." Peter rallies us, leading the charge out the front door.

I follow behind everyone, content to just feel the night air on my skin. There is something magical about the breeze being carried off the ocean, and since this will probably be the only summer I get to vacation like this, I don't want to forget it.

"We call bucket seats!" Jacinda cries.

"I'm the tallest, I get the front seat." Smith calls shotgun.

Except when we get to the cab, which is actually an Escalade, the driver has a bunch of stuff on the front seat, which means the only options are the bucket seats and the back row bench of three. Smith argues with Peter for a second, but in the end loses, and climbs his long body all the way into the back. Heather disappears into the car, and when it's my turn, I see they've left the middle seat in the back row to me.

Which means I'll have to sit directly next to Smith. Great, I can just feel the animosity pouring off him in waves.

I try my hardest to squeeze as close to Heather as I can and don't even bother putting on the seatbelt because that would require him to shift and me to root around just below his butt to find the holder. No, I'd rather risk death than have my hand connect with one of those glorious cheeks of his.

But no matter how far I scoot, it's no use. Smith is just too big and eclipses most of the space. My bare thigh keeps rubbing against the material of his soft cotton summer pants, and I curse Heather for suggesting I wear this. I can feel the heat seeping through the material of his pants on my bare skin, and it takes everything in me to stifle the urge to rub my thighs together.

My cheeks burn in the darkness of the car, because my underwear is slick with desire. Is this simply because it's been so long without Justin? Even before he dumped me a month ago, we hadn't had sex in almost six weeks. I should have known then that something was up, but I was so naive.

The driver turns up the music, some Selena Gomez song that makes any conversation impossible, and I'm happy for that. Sneaking a glance up at Smith, I see he's bent over to the window, trying to escape me, with his nose practically shoved against it.

Of course, he wants no part of sitting next to me.

The fifteen-minute drive is over pretty quickly, and I thank that shot of tequila for giving me the slightest buzz and making it bearable.

It's our first night in the Hamptons, and obviously Heather said we had to join the rest of the housemates in coming out to the bars. I had no objection, because sitting in my room thinking about how I was supposed to share it with Justin is exactly where I don't want to be right now.

We all start at one of the beachside bars, where Peter buys us a round of margaritas and I down mine pretty quickly. With the smell of the ocean, the laughter, small talk, and courage the alcohol gives me, I'm feeling pretty good. Jacinda even falls into a conversation with Heather and me about how work is going, and though job talk is not what I'd love to focus on, it's a start.

Next, we head to a louder bar, one with live music and a crowd that feels halfway to wasted. Another margarita and then a vodka on the rocks has me feeling no pain. Heather and I dance, sing at the top of our lungs, and Peter even makes a cameo on guitar with the band, something I never knew he was so good at.

The whole night has a carefree attitude floating through it—until it doesn't.

"Hey." A guy appears next to me, and my fuzzy brain doesn't comprehend anything but to smile.

I turn back to where Heather is standing to rejoin the conversation, but Random Guy comes into my line of vision again. He's short, not as short as me but just above my eye level, and so not my type. He's blond—also not my type. I don't mean to sound vain, but I've just never been into blond guys, they don't do it for me. Something about a smoldering, brooding dark-haired guy is the thing that gets my heart, and everything south of my waist, galloping.

"I'd like to buy you a drink," he says, whispering in my ear.

Something inside my chest tightens, and it's akin to an internal alarm. Even though this is a crowded bar and it's loud, he's too close. I back up a step.

"Thank you, but I'm okay." I try to give him a reassuring smile and then turn to go again.

That's when I feel a hand on my arm. "Hey, I just want to talk to you."

There is a callous on his palm, and when I go to wrench my arm free like he's scalding me, it roughly scratches against my skin. "No, I'm going to find my friends—"

I'm about to turn and scamper off, even though I can't see any one of the people I came here with, when a towering figure appears in front of me.

"She said no." Smith's voice is directed at Random Guy, but he positions his body almost in front of me.

"Chill, buddy, I didn't realize she had a boyfriend." The guy is drunk, too drunk to notice that he's sorely outmatched when it comes to Smith.

"He's not—" I go to speak up, because the only thing that will make Smith hate me more is if someone assumes he's dating me.

"She's off the market, so move along." Smith is menacing, and his hand hovers just under my elbow, like he might actually touch me.

A shiver of awareness, the kind that his protective approach elicit, runs down my spine. I've forgotten entirely about Random Guy, and I'm openly gaping at Smith. He looks ... *hot*. Like he's about to rip this guy's throat out and then throw me over his shoulder to bring me back to his cave. His chiseled jaw, dotted with dark stubble, tics with fury, and in the neon stage lights I can see his denim blue pupils dilate territorially.

The creep lopes off, probably in search of a girl who will take him up on the offer of a drink, and Smith glares down at me.

Without another word, he turns on his heel and stalks off.

"Hey!" I demand, following him.

But his strides are longer than mine, and in the wedges Heather insisted I wear, it's hard to keep up. I'm pushing past people just as I see him hit the door to exit the bar into the dark, summer night. I follow without hesitation.

"Hey, wait!" I huff out a breath, winded from chasing him.

Smith finally stops, his posture going rigid as he waits for me to catch up with him.

Now that we're out here, alone except for a few smokers and people waiting for rides, I feel so self-conscious.

"Thank you for that back there." I chance looking up at him.

He's scowling into the night, and I wonder if that is his default expression. Maybe just with me, because I saw him laughing and joking tonight with Jacinda and Peter.

"Don't make it a habit. I'm not spending my summer warding off your creeps because you're too nice." His voice cuts me in half.

"Then why did you?" It pops out of my mouth before I can stop it.

Because from the way my tipsy brain is looking at it, he didn't have to come over and help me. In fact, I would have pegged him as laughing at me from the corner, watching this guy try to creepily hit on me.

Smith's indigo eyes smolder as he takes me in. "I didn't need you whining, or gloating, for an entire week that you'd been fawned over by some poor chump. It's bad enough I have to share the same house as you."

Something in me snaps. Not only was I dumped recently, with both my heart and ego taking a significant beating, but I had questioned even coming to the Hamptons in the first place. I'd never done anything to this guy other than try to be freaking nice, and well …

Tequila apparently turns my nerves into steel.

"You're an asshole, you know that? I wouldn't have complained, or even bragged about something positive like a nice man trying to take me out, much less a drunk guy creepily hitting on me in a bar. As if I've ever even confided in you. No, the only thing I've ever tried to do is be cordial, even when you were all but spitting in my face. Did it ever occur to you that maybe it's *me* who thinks sharing a house with *you* is the seventh circle of hell? You sure are a miserable, selfish jerk, Smith."

The guy couldn't look more shocked if I'd slapped him square across the cheek. But I don't wait to hear his biting rebuttal.

I just turn on my wobbly legs and stomp off in search of Heather, with as much dignity and pride as my disheveled, drunken body will allow.

6

SMITH

After a Friday and Saturday night out, Marta decides it would be nice to have Sunday dinner as a house before those of us who have to depart back to the city for the week got on the road.

"Peter, can you slice those potatoes for me?" Marta barks out an order as she tends to the pot she's been stirring for half an hour.

"You sure you want him doing that?" Jacinda snorts.

"He's a doctor, doesn't he have steady hands?" Marta sounds annoyed.

Probably because those of us who hate cooking have been skirting in and out of the kitchen, trying to avoid being taken hostage and given a task.

"Yes, but the man could screw up a bowl of cereal." Jacinda hikes a thumb in the direction of her boyfriend.

"I'll do it," Molly speaks up, stepping away from the chicken she was browning in a skillet.

"You're the best. I can't wait to taste the potato salad. Curry mustard sounds delicious!" Marta smiles so fondly at Molly that I have to turn my back.

She's going overboard with her affections toward Justin's ex this weekend, in an attempt to make her feel included. It must be working, because the two of them have been thick as thieves cooking together all afternoon, dancing to Billy Joel and laughing it up.

Molly tips her head in appreciation. "Thanks, I think it should be good."

I walk out of the room before I say something stupid. There was something about her finally hitting her breaking point on Friday, serving me a piece of her mind, that turned me on more than anything Molly has ever done. I'm attracted to her by instinct, could stare at her for hours. But the way she spoke to me when I pushed her just a bit too far? That had my cock stiffening whenever my mind flitted back to the briefest thoughts of Friday night.

If that little altercation in front of the bar was any indication, Molly won't stand for my shit treatment of her this summer. And that's even more dangerous than the past year, when all she's tried to do is be cordial, in her words.

Because I have a feeling I won't be able to resist feisty Molly. The emotions I've locked away since the first time I saw her are already rattling around in my chest, trying to get free.

"Your bags packed, sucka?" Peter punches me, rather hard, in the bicep.

I pull him into a headlock. Under it all, we're still just those grade school kids being idiots. "Yeah, leaving my bike here and calling a car later."

"You're going to miss a great fucking week," Peter gloats.

"Says the guy who has to go back every Wednesday to see patients until the weekend. You're a moron, plus I'll be back the night *you* have to leave." I flip him the bird.

I have to be back in Manhattan by tomorrow at noon, for a meeting with the interior designer I used for each restaurant we own. She was a genius at creating a space that was both functional, chic, and inviting. The decor of both Mia, our first restaurant, and Il Sole, our second restaurant has been highlighted in almost every review and critique we get. The food at our eateries is sublime, and deserves its own award, but it's not the only reason diners come back. People love atmosphere, especially in this city. They want to feel romantic and alive when they go out to pay for a meal. They want to feel like the room is as abuzz as they feel. It's that electricity you get when dressing up in your favorite outfit on a Friday night, to go spend time with your favorite people after a hard week in the office. That's what we strive for in our restaurants.

And Stefania will be no different, if not a thousand times better. Just hearing the name Campbell and I chose makes me want to collapse with my head in my hands, but I know it's the right thing to do. This restaurant will be a memorial to her, and I'll raise the bar tenfold to make this a place worthy of carrying my sister's name.

"Whatever. Hey, proud of you, man. She would be, too. But if you don't put her favorite fried donuts on the dessert menu, her ghost is going to come down and haunt your ass." He gives a sad, small laugh.

I try to smile, but I think it comes off more like a grimace, because Peter's eyes turn sympathetic. It's been six months since my twin sister was tragically killed, and I still can't talk about her memory with anything but utter grief and fury.

"She did love those fucking donuts," I mutter, thinking about Steph and how she always claimed the last one in the box.

"Men! Dinner is ready!" Heather calls from the back porch.

The women have been cooking all day, and I'm sure I'll be suckered into cleaning up, but I'm too hungry to care at this point.

Peter and I meet Ray, who has appeared from upstairs, at the back door and all file out with beers in our hands.

"Wow, this looks incredible, babe." Ray sits down next to Marta and kisses her cheek in gratitude.

"Thank ya, baby!" She smiles in a bragging way, like she's so proud to provide for him.

"It really does, you guys did a great job," Peter agrees, taking his seat next to Jacinda.

I take the only available chair, which is at the head of the table, with Molly to my right and Heather to my left. I'm not sure if they left this seat for me as a joke, or some kind of offering, but it makes me feel like the Godfather of this table.

"Thank you for cooking," I tell no one in particular.

The spread looks delicious and has my mouth watering. Some kind of spiced chicken, a pasta with some kind of cream sauce, grilled asparagus, a peach and mozzarella salad, and the infamous curried potato salad. The waves clapping on the shore are audible in the distance, and someone hung some kind of fairy lights from the trees near the pool. The ambience is beautiful, and if anything could bring this disjointed cast of characters, it's probably a meal together. Never underestimate the power of good food.

Everyone begins to serve themselves, passing plates around the table for a spoonful of this or a slice of that. The lot of us are quiet as we dig in, and even though I own two Zagat rated restaurants, I have to admit that the food is incredible. Especially the fucking potato salad.

"Wow, Molly, this potato salad." Peter groans as he shovels another forkful in.

"I could seriously eat this all day. I make her make it for me every time she comes over." Heather grins through a bite.

Molly shrugs, blushing under the praise. "Well, thank you. It's my mother's recipe, so I can't take credit."

"Do your parents live in New York, Molly? I don't think I ever asked." Jacinda wipes her mouth and politely addresses Justin's ex-girlfriend.

The truth is, I don't think any of us talked to Molly much one-on-one while she was with Justin. My best friend is larger than life, the talker in a big crowd, the guy who draws an entire room to his vivacious story. She was eclipsed in his shadow, something I noticed often and secretly hated him for.

Molly smiles, as if she's thinking of her parents. "I grew up in New Jersey, in Linden. They're still there, in the little ranch on East Street. It's just the three of us, and if I have time, I try to go visit once a month."

I knew she was from close by, but I didn't realize she grew up in New Jersey. I don't know anything about it there, but I wonder suddenly what her childhood was like.

"Isn't it weird to go back and visit your childhood home?" Marta muses.

"*Yes*," Heather blurts out, and then starts cracking up. "About a year ago, I was dating this guy, and I brought him home to meet my parents. I remember he wanted to get busy in my childhood bedroom, but I couldn't go through with it. There was nothing turning me on about Jesse McCartney and Chad Michael Murray posters staring at my twin bed."

Peter booms out a laugh. "Oh God, *yes*."

"Peter's childhood bedroom has this permanent hockey bag smell, I can't even sleep in there." Jacinda chuckles.

"When I stay at Marta's parent's place, they make me sleep in the basement." Ray smiles into his plate.

"That's cold," Peter says.

"No sex before marriage, that's what my parents think." Marta snorts, because we all know her parents thinking she's a virgin is straight up delusion.

"If I went back to my parent's place, I'd have to sleep on the lumpy pull out couch. I always beg off, even on Christmas." I smirk.

"How many siblings do you have again?" Heather asks me curiously.

"Seven," I say, before the thought hits me. "Uh ... six. I was one of eight."

The whole table goes quiet, and that cloud of misery I've been trying to shake for six months looms close over my head.

"You have to go back to the city tonight?" Jacinda pipes up, saving me from myself.

"Yeah, I have some stuff going on at my new restaurant this week." I try to inject as much cheeriness as a guy like me can muster into my tone.

"Who else is going back tonight?" She peers around the table.

Molly raises a finger, as if to say she is, too, and Ray clears his throat. "I'm going back tomorrow afternoon. Should be back on Thursday."

"Why don't you let Molly ride back in your car? You're both going to the city," Marta suggests, and I wish the glare I give her could melt flesh.

I'm about to protest, or extend a very rigid invitation to share my car, when Molly pipes up. "Oh no, that's okay. I was going to browse some of the shops before the Jitney arrives, have to get my mom a little something. She's never been out here, and she'd just love something from one of the antique shops in town."

It sounds so sincere, I almost believe it, but I know that the items in those shops cost thousands of dollars, even for something as small as a salt shaker.

The rest of dinner goes off without a hitch, the conversation flowing smoothly and not delving into topics that are any deeper than surface level.

I'm glad when my car arrives at eight and I get a full two

hours of quiet by myself. I'm not the most extroverted person to begin with, and spending the weekend in a house with six other people is something I've barely done since I was a kid.

Growing up, my house was a zoo, with kids and relatives always popping up, and noise always at the highest volume.

It's why I cherish my thousand-square-foot bachelor pad even more now. I know how hard I've worked for it, and when I arrive home around ten thirty, I'm greeted by pure and utter silence.

7

MOLLY

In the end, I do visit some of the local boutiques before the eight p.m. Jitney arrives.

Though, I buy nothing, because who can afford a beach blanket that costs seven thousand dollars? That's more than I spend on rent for half the year.

But it was a good excuse not to ride the two hours back to the city in the same car as Smith, and I got to listen to the audiobook that's been in my to-be-read pile for forever, so I count it as a win.

And while the weekend was a godsend for my nerves and self-care, it's Monday morning and right back to the grind.

"Come here and let me put your suntan lotion on," I call to Rudy, an eight-year-old splashing in the creek of Central Park.

"Mol, did you grab those morning snacks?" one of the co-counselors in my group yells over the heads of dozens of campers.

"In the cooler. There are cheese sticks and apple slices, and then everyone gets a water," I tell her while rubbing thick white lotion onto Rudy's arms.

My summers are usually even more hectic than the rest of

my year. Aside from this two-month period, where I've given myself a slight break to enjoy the spoils of life that I never really experienced, I usually work myself to the bone in the summer.

As a fifth grade teacher at a school located in an impoverished community in a low-income part of the city, I obviously don't do my job for the money. Half the time, I barely break even with the salary from my day job, and I put so much of that money back into books and resources for my students that the school can't afford or provide. And I don't mind doing that at all. On the contrary, I'd honestly do my job for free if money was no object and I didn't need to pay bills or live. The things I'm able to do for my students, the couple who really blossom with undivided attention and compassion, it's all worth it.

But, unfortunately, I do need to pay bills to be able to keep living in the city and making a difference. So I hustle in the summer. I've worked at the same summer camp, run inside Central Park, for the last five years. And on top of that, I wait tables like crazy. I also wait tables during the school year, but only on weekends so that I can get all of my school work and grading done. In the summer, I could work five eight-hour waitressing shifts on top of my summer camp work.

Typically, I'm exhausted and run ragged during the summers, and Justin had finally convinced me to take some time to unwind and live out my life in the year I turned thirty. Part of me hates him now, because I'm missing out on making so much money, but part of me is happy I took the leap.

Last weekend in the Hamptons, aside from the Smith drama, was really wonderful. Exploring the beach with Heather, going out to new places, getting out of the turbulence of the city. I can even tell that I'm more relaxed with my campers and my fellow waitstaff this week during my return to Manhattan.

"So, how was your weekend?" Bobby, one of the counselors assigned to our group, sits down on the bench next to me.

We watch like hawks while our forty or so campers, policed by six of us counselors, frolic in this designated area of the park during their free time. After this, we'll walk over to the area that's been set up for today's craft, a draw your own portrait station. The camp is for the kids of this city's elite and pays like you would imagine it does. Most of the kids are great, attentive and yearning to both play and learn. There are the occasional few who know how spoiled they are and just what they're allowed to get away with at home. But overall, it's fun working with kids younger than my normal eleven-year-olds. Most of the time, I have five- and six-year-old-girls who want me to braid their hair and tell them stories about their dolls.

"Amazing." I sigh. "Just what the breakup doctor ordered."

Bobby sniffs jealously. "Girl, I am so envious. You got rid of the asshole boyfriend and still got to go on his trip. You're winning. Now if you'll only let me take you out on the town this week."

We've worked together every summer for the last three years, so Bobby knows me well. And he's always trying to make me come out with him to his latest gay club or drag show. I'm not a partier by any standards and knowing there is a chance I could get called up on stage during one of those shows? Yeah, no. My embarrassment meter would bust and I'd probably faint.

I shake my head. "You know it will always be a no."

He leans in, a juicy smile on his face. "Tell me you got laid this weekend."

That makes me chuckle. "Since when do I strike you as the girl to go on vacation and suddenly start having one-night stands?"

He rolls his eyes, slumping on the bench. "Come on, Molly! You're supposed to be letting me live vicariously through you this summer. And single me would be all over the man meat in the Hamptons. Seriously, there wasn't anyone?"

My mind flashes back to Smith, and I must give myself away, because he smacks me on the arm.

"Spill it!"

I huff in annoyance. "There really is no one. I just got into a fight with Justin's best friend, the one I told you about?"

"Hottie McHotstick? Um, can you explain why you're not all up in bone town with that demigod now that your ex is flaunting around in Asia?"

The way he puts things makes me almost spit out the sip of Gatorade I just took. "You're too much. Um, not that I want to go to bone town with anyone anytime soon, still in breakup city over here. But that would never happen. The guy looks at me like I'm gum stuck to the bottom of his shoe."

"Miss Molly, I have to go poop." One of my five-year-olds comes up and tugs on my hand.

"*And* that's my cue." I grin at Bobby.

"Don't think a little poop is going to derail me. My mission for you this summer is the demigod. If I can't have him, you will, and then you'll tell me all about it. Plus, I didn't hear anything in there that said you didn't want him *not* to offer."

The smirk on Bobby's face can only be characterized as the cat who ate the canary.

But he's right. Never once did I say that I wouldn't entertain the idea if Smith did come to me and offer.

8

SMITH

There are blueprints spread over the makeshift work bench of a two-by-four propped up on two sawhorses.

I'm pouring over them, putting each detail to memory, when Campbell walks over with two glasses of what smells like Scotch.

I raise an eyebrow at him. "It's only four."

He shrugs, his big, bulky frame sitting in a folding chair next to the makeshift table. He hands me the highball, which I don't refuse, and then tips his shaved blond head back and takes a big sip.

My business partner is an ex-Navy SEAL with a shrewd eye for numbers and a surprisingly large tolerance for bullshit conversation. Of the two of us, he is the schmoozer, though he's also the brains of the financial operation behind our restaurants. I'm the one who gets his hands dirty, who constructs and helps design from the studs up. I'm the half with an eerily good sense of great chefs and waitstaff, and I do my homework each and every week on industry food trends or up-and-coming products. Together, our partnership is a solid one.

Though, we're having a setback today.

"If they don't give us this liquor license, we could just sneak highball glasses to each patron's table. Call it prohibition-style dining," Campbell jokes.

"They're going to give us that license if I have to chain myself to city hall," I quip, taking a drink myself.

The scotch burns, but it clears my head. I forgot how much bullshit there is to deal with when opening a restaurant. We haven't done it in almost two years, and I'm getting a migraine with how much shit is on my plate.

"Maybe I should just stay here through the weekend," I pose the option.

He shakes his head, grimacing through a sip of liquor. "No, you have to go. You need a fucking break, man. I got this."

I nod, because we've already had this argument. Back at the beginning of the year, when we were trying to buy this space after Stephanie passed, I'd been in a bad place. As months went by, Campbell convinced me to take the summer part-time, and I'd pushed back so hard.

But after a full on breakdown one weekend in March, which could have had something to do with Justin pondering asking Molly to move in or marry him, I fully committed to the Hamptons house. And I can't deny that being by the water this weekend did help me feel marginally better.

Suddenly, the front door of the restaurant, which is just two pieces of swinging plywood, bursts open and three chatting tornadoes of opinion and energy come charging in.

"Smithy, you here?" I hear my aunt's thick Brooklyn accent, and I'm jumping up.

"Ma, Aunt Lorraine, Suzie, you can't just come in here!" I bark at them, but no one is listening to me.

My mother, her sister, and my first cousin all squawk about, looking at the restaurant that is still just sheetrock and construction zone.

"Doesn't look like much has been accomplished, Smith." Ma gives me a skeptical look.

"Ma, we only just bought the lot three months ago. Construction only started two weeks ago. It's going to take a while." I don't even know why I'm trying to explain any of this, as none of them are going to listen to me.

They all come up and kiss me hastily on the cheek, before clucking over to Campbell and flitting about him.

"Oh, Campbell, you're such a handsome boy," my aunt Lorraine coos.

Suzie, who is ten years older than me with a husband and three kids of her own, bats her lashes at him. "When are you going to come over so I can cook you a proper meal?"

Mom brushes some dirt off the collar of his shirt, and I'm surprised she doesn't lick her thumb to rub a smudge off his cheek. He just chuckles, having been very acquainted with how my family operates.

Being one of eight kids is like being a circus animal these days. When people find out, everyone oohs and aahs at you like you literally might be hiding a tail in your pants or something. It's just not heard of, especially for people who live in New York City, but I'm a testament that it happens.

Coming from a big Italian family, chaos and loud relatives are my normal. I'm one of eight kids, with four aunts on my mom's side and three uncles on my dad's Italian slash Irish side. Don't let the Irish last name fool you, we're full-blooded pasta and wine consumers, with a flair for dramatics and the need to be up in every single person's business.

I grew up on the same street or down the block from my twenty first cousins, I've got three nieces and a nephew, and that doesn't even include the extended family who show up to every Christmas, graduation party, or christening. When my oldest sister, Valerie, got married, there were four hundred people at the wedding.

"Why haven't you been home yet? You've been back in the city for three days?" my mom insists, walking up to me with her hands already near my face.

I scrub a hand over my face. "I've been a little busy, Ma. I'll try to get over tomorrow."

"Your father had a doctor's appointment, would have been nice if you could have taken him." She scowls.

"No one told me had an appointment, or I would have put it in my schedule." I sigh.

For some reason, every member of my family expected this psychic ability to read each other's brains and show up at all hours of the day, especially for things like dance recitals and doctor's appointments.

"The boy has too much money, it's making him selfish." Aunt Lorraine looks me up and down, sniffing judgmentally.

"I'm right here, Aunt Lorraine." I wave my arms, as if my presence isn't completely oblivious.

Suzie just hides a chuckle behind her hand, because all of us kids have been subjected to this Italian guilt our entire lives.

"Show me the plans," Ma insists, completely switching topics as if she hasn't just accused me of not showing up for her and Dad.

I walk over to the blueprints with just her, away from the other three people standing in this dusty, dirty construction zone.

Pointing to the architectural designs, I begin to explain,

"We're putting in this sleek long bar against the front wall, right when you walk in. We want it to be kind of a fusion place.

Of course, we'll have sit down tables with a stacked menu, but we want it to be a lounge as well. Somewhere people will want to hang out all night, with a killer bar. And then over there we'll have a massive fireplace, with pictures of the whole family in black-and-white stretching all the way up to the ceiling. There will be exposed brick, we're trying to use a lot of the original structure since it's so historic and beautiful."

I point out a few more elements, and I know I'll be consulting with her soon on the menu. My mother is the best cook I know, and she learned it all from her own relatives back in Italy. She's helped with every single menu I've ever put together.

Mom pats my cheek. "She would be so proud of this place. You're doing a good thing, Smithy."

I see it then, the abject pain in her eyes. My mother doesn't talk much about Stephanie's death, or the time surrounding it. But I heard her one night when I'd gone over to spend time with the family, maybe a month after the accident, crying to Dad in the kitchen.

"How do I live now, Francis? I'm a mother, I was supposed to go first. I'm not supposed to see my baby leave this earth."

I never thought about it like that, I had been too wrapped up in my own pain at first. But I can't imagine how devastated she feels waking up day after day if I know how much pain I still carry.

"All right." She sighs a shaky breath, turning to smile at her sister and niece. "Let's get a move on. Diana has a bake sale at the church and I have to drop off the muffins in my car."

That was my mother. I don't think the woman sat still for any second of the day. She was always moving or helping someone.

They all kiss Campbell and me, then whirl out as fast as they blew in.

"Jesus, your family is nuts." He smirks, sipping the last of his scotch.

"You're not lying." I laugh, trying to get my head back into work.

I only have one more day before I head back to the Hamptons for a straight week, and I need to get as much in as possible.

9

MOLLY

"Thank you for dining with us, I hope you folks have a great night."

I give the table of elderly couples my brightest smile, since they were my best diners tonight. And secretly, I'm crossing my fingers behind my back, hoping they leave a hefty tip.

"You were wonderful, darling. Now go get off your shift, you deserve a little fun." One of the old women pats my hand kindly, winking as if she got up to some trouble when she was my age.

Taking that as my cue to leave them to the bill, and hopefully have her push her husband to giving me a twenty-five percent tip or higher, I skirt around other tables and waiters to the back of Aja. It's a French-Japanese fusion restaurant that serves fish dishes for fifty bucks a pop and has a wine list longer and more expensive than my monthly bills. I landed the job here two summers ago, and I wait tables for them on and off during the school year, too.

Out of all my restaurant jobs, Aja is by far the best paying, though it's the most challenging. Since it's so high end, that means no notepads, which means memorizing the rotating menu of intricate dishes their Michelin chef puts together. I need to know the fluctuating price of certain wine bottles, and how to properly uncork table side. We serve the best sake in the city, and I have to brush up on my knowledge about that every once in a while. Not to mention the proper way to set a table, which side of a guest to put a plate down on, and just being "on" for all the patrons.

People think being a waitress is easy, but exhausting, and it's anything but. At some of these upscale places in the city, it seriously takes a four-year degree to get a job on the serving staff. Plus a headshot—no, I'm not kidding. I had to have Heather take a professional shot of me when I submitted my résumé to Aja.

"Hey, you getting out of here?" Delaney, the head waitress who has been here nearly ten years, asks me.

"Just cashed out my last table." I pull my half-apron off from around my waist. "It was a crazy night. I had that twelve-top, and then the table of bankers who kept trying to proposition me."

Delaney rolls her eyes. "I hate those kinds of tables. It's like, this isn't a strip joint. You could go to one of those if you want tits and avoid the hundred-dollar lobster dinner here."

I crack up. "I know, I don't get it. Can you count my tips?"

Giving her the pouch I always keep on me until the end of the night, she counts them, and then goes to the computer to reference my credit card transactions. Pulling open the cash drawer, Delaney counts some bills and then hands them to me.

"A four-hundred-dollar night, impressive." She tips her head in acknowledgment to me.

Inside, I do a fist pump. That's a great tip night, and Lord knows I need it.

"You off somewhere fun?" she asks.

I shrug. "Home to sleep. But I'm headed back to the Hamptons tomorrow morning for a few days. I have that house share this summer, remember?"

She sighs wistfully. "How could I forget. Lucky bitch."

"Hey, you're going to the Hamptons? I'm leaving tonight, you want a ride?" Kirsten, one of the bartenders, passes me while listening to our conversation.

We're not exactly friends, but it's nice that she's offering. Plus, it would mean avoiding the Jitney and waking up to the sound of the surf.

"Are you sure? I wouldn't want to make you leave earlier or anything," I ask.

She shakes her head and waves me off. "No problem, I have a bartending gig tonight at one of the beach bars, so I have to go anyway. We'll be there late, but I have an extra seat. Having company on the drive is always nice."

I'm not one to pass up a free ride, and it seems like she doesn't mind. "Sure, that would be great. I'll pay for gas."

"Great, can you meet me back here in an hour?"

Checking my watch, that's just enough time to go home, shower the Aja smell off me, and pack a quick bag. "I'll be here."

An hour later, I'm packing my small duffel into the back of Kirsten's car, and then two hours after that, she's dropping me in the driveway of my summer house share.

"Thank you so much, I owe you big time," I tell her.

"Seriously, not a problem. If you ever need a ride and I'm headed down, let me know. I hate driving by myself."

I nod, closing the passenger door, and smile to myself. I haven't talked often with Kirsten at the restaurant, but she's a cool girl, and it was nice to get to know her more.

The house is pretty closed up and quiet as I let myself in the front door with my key, and I assume everyone is either in their own rooms, asleep, or out partying. The first floor is clean save for some empty Amazon boxes, and as I pass through the kitchen, there is a plate of scones and some open wine bottles on the island.

Walking up the stairs, I try to tiptoe, in case anyone is sleeping.

As I pass Marta and Ray's door, I think I hear moaning from inside. I duck my head, blushing, because something inside me burns for that kind of intimacy right now.

It's been a long time since I had that kind of pleasure, and I'm ashamed to admit that Justin was a jealous lover and I let him be. There were many times I didn't orgasm, and I never said anything. I hate that I'm *that* woman, the one too insecure to tell a man what she likes during sex. But Justin, he was just so overpowering in a personality sense. I wanted to please him in every way, because when I had that affection it felt better than anything.

Peter and Lucinda's door is closed, but there is no sound behind it, and I wonder if they went out. I know Heather is out at some bar, because she texted me.

I won't let myself think about Smith, plus I don't have to pass his door. It's at the end of the hallway, one past mine, and I turn into my room so fast. I don't want to think about whether he's sleeping in there, what he sleeps in, or if there is a girl occupying his bed.

I shake my head to clear it and set my duffel down. I make quick work of unpacking and then slip into my ocean and starfish printed pajama set. When it comes to sleep attire, I get the most juvenile kind, but it's so comfortable. The tank top and shorts feel like the inside of a fleece sweatshirt, and the turquoise and pink pattern remind me of a beach town.

It's almost midnight when I'm about to dive straight for my pillows, but realize I have to go to the bathroom. Only Smith and I share one, because every other bedroom has its own en suite, and I plan to tiptoe out to it directly across from my bedroom door.

But as I go to turn into the hallway, I'm nearly knocked to the floor. My side and back collide with something impossibly solid, and then two big hands wrap around my arms just as my heart ricochets into my throat, pulling me upright.

"Jesus, fuck, you scared the shit out of me!" Smith hisses, and my nerves pulse erratically all over my body.

Not only because I was bracing myself for the impact of a fall, but also because Smith, naked in every way save for a black pair of boxer briefs, has his fingers no more than two inches away from my nipples.

Which are completely bare of a bra, the only material between them and the hallway air is my thin pajama top. And at this vantage point, Smith is looking straight down said top.

"I'm ... sorry, I didn't, I thought ..." I stutter, trying to form a sentence.

"When did you even get back here? I thought everyone was asleep or out." His tone is all accusation, and he still hasn't let go of me.

We're so close, dangerously close, and I can feel the wetness start to build in my underwear. Smith is six and a half feet of gorgeous, toned man muscle, and even in this dark hallway, I'm getting an eyeful. Lord, I'm eye level with his abs, and if I snuck a glance down, I could see how well he fills out those boxers.

"I caught a ride with a friend after my restaurant shift. I wanted to wake up to the ocean," I explain, as if that's the detail he was looking for.

His impossibly blue-black eyes turn curious. "You wait tables?"

Shame burns my gut, because I just gave him one more thing to hold against me. "Yes, unfortunately I cannot get by on just a teacher's salary."

Might as well make the observation before he does it for me, in a ruder manner.

"Where do you work?" he asks, and I can feel it as his thumb starts to rub slowly up and down the back of my arm where he's holding it.

I have to catch my knees from buckling at the sensation, and I swear, my eyes almost roll back into my head. I'm not even sure he's doing it, but to me, it feels like full-on seduction to my sex-deprived body.

"Aja," I tell him, knowing I'll regret it later but unable to keep my mouth shut with what he's doing to my heart and my brain.

He nods. "Good place."

Our eyes lock, and for a split second, I think he might kiss me. His face looms ever closer, and my mouth goes dry at the thought of how much passion he must pack behind those lips. His declaration on New Year's Eve, when he told me that I wouldn't know passion if it smacked me in the mouth, haunts me to this day.

But something must click in his brain, and then he lets me go, stepping back.

"Don't go sneaking around the hallways again. You're going to give someone a heart attack."

Then he's turning his back, retreating to his room. The last sight I'm given is a flash of the two perfectly sculpted globes in his boxers before the light from his room is cut off in the dark hallway.

I slump against the wall, breathing heavy.

How the hell am I going to get a good night's sleep with the memory of his hands on my skin?

10

SMITH

The white linen curtains in my room blow open with the breeze, and I'm itching to get out into the sunlight.

I tossed and turned last night, thinking about the petite school teacher the next room over. Jesus Christ, how was I supposed to get any shut eye when Molly was prancing around in those paper thin pajamas? And when I touched her?

It's the first time I've ever felt her skin, aside from the forced pleasantry of a hand shake or a hug we've shared very rarely over the last year. Everything in me wanted to capture her mouth in that dark hallway, and I nearly did. But what would that lead to? I am in no place to treat her the way she deserves, and she's just broken up with my best friend. She was all but off-limits when it came to bro code, even if Justin wasn't here.

Pulling on a pair of swim trunks, I head downstairs, hoping someone has already made breakfast or packed the coolers for the beach.

"Oh, you're an angel." I kiss Jacinda good morning on the cheek as I spot the spread of eggs and waffles she prepared.

She swats my butt. "Only because I had a hankering for

chocolate chip waffles. Don't think this will be a regular thing, we're not dating."

"Hell, it's not even a regular thing for me," Peter pipes up from the table, looking sweaty in his tennis outfit.

"You hit around this morning?" I ask, coming to sit next to him with a plate full of food.

He nods. "Yep, the court is awesome, we should play a little doubles game."

"Not with me." Jacinda snorts. "The only exercise I'm doing this summer is rolling over to get my other side tan."

"I'll play!" Marta walks into the kitchen in a fire engine red bikini.

She and Jacinda hug, and they compare bathing suits, complimenting each other in that ridiculous way that women do where they go on and on as if they're at a sleepover.

"Sold. We should set up some kind of bet for this game. Loser has to clean toilets. Oh! Or buy us all lobsters." Peter slaps the table.

"I could get behind that." I sip my coffee, loving the relaxed feeling that settles over me.

When I got back to the Hamptons two days ago, I was wound up. Things at the new restaurant weren't going to plan—they never did, but it meant more with this project—and my family was on my last nerve. I'm glad to be back here for a week straight, because I finally feel as though I can take a deep breath.

"Molly, do you play tennis?" Marta asks, and my head shoots up.

Molly walks farther into the kitchen, and I swear I almost swallow my tongue. She's more modest than the other two women in the room, but in a sleek navy blue one-piece, there is too much that can be left to the imagination. I wonder if she has freckles on the skin I can't see, and whether or not her belly button dips in the way I've dreamed it does. As she walks around the island to collect a small plate of breakfast food, my eyes are glued to her ass. The style of the suit isn't one of those new ones all the girls wear, with their cheeks all but exposed. No, Molly covers it up, and I'm left salivating over the tease of a round globe and the hint of a wax underneath.

I have to shift in my seat, because my dick is suddenly rock hard in a room full of people at nine in the morning.

"I've dabbled. My campers would say I'm a pro, though I can barely serve the ball." She chuckles in a self-deprecating way.

"Well, there, we have our fourth. We're going to play a doubles match, you can play with Smith and I'll play with Peter. Loser buys the house a lobster dinner."

My hackles go up, and I'm about to make a quip about how I'd have to shell out for the lobsters if we lost, but Molly beats me to it.

"Yeah right, Smith would intentionally throw the game and then stick me with a lobster bill, just to see if I could pay it." She snorts.

The whole room goes silent, and then everyone aside from me starts howling with laughter.

"Holy shit, she just handed you your ass." Peter points at me.

"Damn, girl, you got balls. I like you more than I thought I did." Jacinda goes up to pat her on the back.

Meanwhile, I'm floored that she just nailed me like that in front of *my* friends. I grumble something unintelligible while everyone has a good old laugh on my behalf.

"Who wants to hit the beach?" Heather comes in, picking up nothing but a cup of coffee.

She's the type of chick I'd usually date, but something about it feels off to me. Probably because the woman I've fallen in love with before I even knew her last name is also staying in this house. But also because I've been severely limiting my dating life in not only the past year, but the past six months.

Since the night I met Molly, I seem to compare every single female to her. And then after Stephanie died, there was no point in trying to form connections I knew would never last.

"Me!" Molly throws her hand up.

"I'll grab a football or something," Peter tells me, and I nod.

The seven of us work together to get coolers packed, towels in bags, and a whole slew of beach entertainment is carted with us down to the strip of sand just outside our backyard. Silently, I thank Justin for finding a house right on the ocean, even if it does cost a little bit more for the summer. Not having to pack up cars and drag all the heavy shit to the sand just to pack it all back up an hour later, or to find a bathroom, is pretty sweet.

Once we get down there, Ray and I set up the massive tent Marta bought online, and position the chairs under there for the people who don't want to lie in the sun. Heather unpacks a bunch of drinks, and Peter pulls out several different balls for us to throw around. Immediately after everything is somewhat assembled, I run for the ocean. I've always loved the sea, and diving in headfirst is something I've been looking forward to after the busy couple days I had back in the city.

After a while, the rest of the crew decides to go on a long walk down the beach, but I'm far too comfortable and lazy to join them. The lull of the sun and the hypnotic rhythm of the sea rock me off into a daydream-like state, where I'm not sleeping but I'm not exactly lucid.

By the time I sit up to grab a drink of water, I see that it's just Molly and me in our group's little beach area setup. She's three towels over, in a lounge beach chair, completely lost in a book. Her sun hat flops down over her forehead, shading her eyes and the pages of her story from the sun.

She looks adorable and with the way she's chewing on her lip; I want to go over there and throw that book down in the sand.

"What are you reading?" The question pops out before I can stop it.

Molly lowers her head slowly, but can't seem to pull her eyes off the page, as if she's screen locked on the book. "Hm?"

Twisting the cap off one of the flavored, sparkling waters Heather threw in the cooler, I decide to ask again. "What are you reading?"

This time, she fully looks up at me, blinking, as if she can't believe I just asked. "*Jane Eyre.*"

I nod. "Never read it. It looks like you're enjoying it."

Again, Molly stares at me as if I might crack a rude obscenity at any moment. "It's one of my favorites, I've read it at least a dozen times."

"Really? Why re-read it?" I'm genuinely curious, because I barely read books once.

I'm too busy, and if I'm not working, I'm usually asleep or catching the rare sports games. The most I read these days are food critic reviews, Michelin nominations, Zagat guide books, and the menus for my own restaurants.

She shrugs self-consciously. "Because I love it. It's one of my favorites."

"What is it about?" I press, knowing that I'm flirting with danger.

This is the first normal conversation we've probably ever had, and the fact that we're on a beach, alone, has me feeling bold. I'm dropping my defenses, and if I'm not careful, everything I feel for her is going to start rolling out.

"It's about a woman living in nineteenth century England, and her abusive childhood that leads into a life of teaching. She comes to live as a governess in a wealthy man's home, and he's brute and harsh. Eventually, she sees his softer side, and they fall in love despite the flaws in each of them."

The way she describes it, in such a romantic, breathless way, has my heart catching in my chest.

Is this the kind of love she wishes for? Does she imagine that a man so brute and harsh could reveal himself to her? I sound like a sap, but the way Molly speaks about this book has me sitting up a little taller on my towel.

"Sounds familiar," I mutter under my breath.

"What's that?" Her hat blows up in the wind, and she catches it before it flies off.

"Nothing. Do you think they'll be back soon?" I pretend to look down the beach in search of them, because it hurts to look at her any longer.

Sitting here, acting normal, it gives me a glimpse into what I could have with her. I wonder if she's ever considered me that way, but the gnawing burn and ache in my gut knows that she still only sees that with Justin.

He's been gone for a month, and I swear I heard her crying in her room the other night.

I'm in love with my best friend's girl, and there isn't a damn thing I can do to make her see that I'm the one she should be with.

11

MOLLY

"Turn the music up!" Heather demands, and Peter obeys. She's standing on a barstool pushed out from the kitchen island, shaking her hips to a Rihanna song, shouting the words at the top of her lungs.

The rest of the housemates follow along in a drunken sort of fancy, Jacinda is gyrating with a glass of white wine in her hand, Peter has been downing whiskey all night, and Marta and Ray are all but dry humping at the kitchen table.

Everyone is pretty wasted after a night out at one of the most popular Montauk bars, and I'm not too far behind them.

"Have another shot!" Heather points at me, and then to a bottle of vodka.

I hold up my hands in protest. "It's almost two in the morning, it's not time for more shots!"

I've already had plenty of vodka sodas, and I'm barely standing up straight.

"Oh, come on, coward! Have another shot!" Smith taunts me.

He's even let loose tonight, and is drunker than I've seen him ... hell, maybe ever.

"If you're such a big, *strong* man, you take one!" I push the bottle toward him.

We're all acting like college kids, and we'll have the thirty-something hangovers to prove it in the morning. But right now, we feel invincible.

He squares his shoulders and gives me a smug grin. "Anything you can do, I can do better."

My head tips back with laughter. "God, you're a child!"

When he slides a shot glass my way, I tip it back without even cheers-ing him. I'm that petty and want to show him how wrong he is. The alcohol burns my throat and I know I might be paying for this with a trip to pray to the porcelain god in the wee hours of the morning, but I'm drunk enough to not let him win.

"Dance, monkeys!" Heather shouts as she kicks off a high-heeled sandal, and it goes flying across the room.

"Is it time for bed?" Jacinda whines, hanging her arms around Peter's neck.

"We're going to bed!" Marta calls as Ray all but drags her from the room.

"Great, we'll have to hear her moaning all night again. I need to get laid." Heather slumps onto her stool as the music stops.

"Me too." Smith hiccups and then chuckles at himself.

For a split second, I watch as Heather's eyes wander over to him, and an intense jealously burns a hole in the lining of my stomach.

What the hell? I really must be drunker than I thought, because who am I to care if they sleep together? I want Heather to get some, even if I can't, and Smith is not mine.

Even though he was nicer than he's ever been to me down on that beach today. And even though I've been having vivid daydreams about his lips, and what he might do to me in that dark hallway when no one is looking …

But I'm not ready for all of that. Nor do I want to just *get laid*.

The truth is, I'm still brokenhearted. I was with Justin for a little over a year. That's a long time to spend with one person. You learn a lot about them, develop a routine, and fall into a nice rhythm of like with them. That's what we had; I'd spend the night at his place from Thursday to Sunday. I would cook him dinner on Monday nights. We had a weekly movie night, and would often jog on Saturday mornings in Central Park. I knew all of his quirks, or so I thought I did.

Justin was the guy for me, *again*, or so I thought. I thought we were going to end up moving in together and getting married. I envisioned our future together, and then he just completely completely chopped that vision up with a machete. It doesn't mean I'm not trying to pick up the tattered pieces now that he's gone. He left over a month ago, and while the sharp, needling pain of a fresh breakup doesn't live inside me anymore, there is still that ache I can't ditch.

I'm reminded every time I step foot in the summer house, a place we were supposed to grow stronger in. Each time I cook myself a meal, alone in my apartment, a tiny stab hits me in the center of my chest. Maybe it isn't so much the guy I miss, because let's be honest, he was a dick for a lot longer than I chose to realize it. But I miss the stability and comfort of a long-term relationship, and I'm still grieving that.

"Are you going to puke tonight?" Heather directs the question at me, because she knows my history with hangovers.

I shrug, too drunk to be embarrassed in front of Smith. "Maybe."

He grimaces, completely in on our conversation. "Do it out your window then. Don't stink up our bathroom."

Our bathroom. Even though we only share it since our rooms are right next door to one another, that word does funny things to my stomach when associated with Smith and me.

"Maybe I'll do it right now," I challenge him, and then race off up the stairs.

I hear the scraping of chair legs as I round the corner to the second floor, but get to the bathroom and lock it before he can fight me for it. We've been avoiding each other in this hallway ever since the night I got back and tiptoeing around who uses the bathroom first or second is part of that.

Only three seconds later, there is a banging on the door that rattles the hinges.

"You better not be puking in there!" Smith growls.

"All over your precious hairbrush and expensive cologne!" I yell through the plywood.

"Molly!"

The way he says my name, in that angry but teasing tone, has all of my pink parts standing at attention.

I take my time washing my face, brushing my teeth, and pulling my hair out of its clip to brush it. Part of me wishes I changed into my pajamas first, so I could crawl right into bed, but I'm stupidly cocky that I got first dibs on the bathroom tonight.

When I'm done putting my night moisturizer on, I survey the sink. And spot the flecks of toothpaste, Smith's toothbrush, and even an errant piece of used floss. All things I've asked him politely to clean up before.

"Can you stop leaving your toothbrush and paste on the sink?" I ask when I finally open the door.

His big body is crowding the doorjamb, and I wish those top two buttons on his shirt weren't undone. It's making it very hard to concentrate on anything else.

"Got a problem with that?" His tone is half-annoyed, half-mocking.

Typically, I'd never square off with him, but he's a grown man. He doesn't need to dirty up the bathroom we're sharing.

The least he could do is wash off the rim of the sink when he spits his gross used toothpaste everywhere.

I finish applying my ChapStick, and then turn to him, trying to roll my shoulders back and appear the more dominant person in this conversation.

"Actually, yes. It's a shared space, and I don't like having to either clean up the mess or place my things around it. I'm simply asking for you to wipe it off before you finish your night or morning routine."

There, that sounded fair.

He reaches over, so close to me, and plucks my ChapStick off the sink. Pulling off the cap as he keeps full eye contact with me, he proceeds to smear the vanilla-flavored balm on his lips.

My jaw is practically on the floor, both turned on and disgusted that he's using my product, the one I just put on my own mouth.

"Noted." He grins, like the devil he is.

I want to smack him in his gorgeous face. My cheeks are flaming, I feel them, and I'm so mad that I can't form a sentence. My silence allows him to escape, and as is typical in this situation, all the comebacks I should have said come flooding my brain about three minutes too late.

It's funny how every time we interact, with each instance I come in contact with Smith, I forget all about my broken heart.

And start wondering what it would be like if it beat for him.

12

MOLLY

There is something about New York City in the summer.

The rich crowd, or those who can scrounge up enough money for a house share, insist that the best thing to do when the warmer months hit Manhattan is to flee it. And while I get the certain perks about that, since it's my first summer experiencing that exodus, there is a nostalgic, quieter feel to the city on summer weekends.

I live in the Murray Hill area of the city, on the fifth of a five-floor walk-up. My apartment is the size of a shoebox, it doesn't heat or cool well, and I pay an arm and a leg for it. But it's home. I don't have to share it. And it's easily accessible from all parts of the city.

As I walk along the streets of my neighborhood, out for a rare Saturday afternoon stroll, I listen to a podcast interviewing one of my favorite authors at a low volume. There is an important private party at Aja tonight, and the tips to be made were too good to turn down. So I stayed back from the Hamptons this weekend, and I'm enjoying an hour off from life, something I don't get often.

The streets are practically bare, aside from the errant taxi or millennial brunchers. It's too early in the day for the drinking crowd yet, and most of the families who actually buy in this neighborhood are at their summer homes after the workweek ended.

It's magical, this city at a dull whisper. Of course, it's never quiet, but the charm of the old brick buildings or townhome fronts shows more when there aren't hordes of people and honking. I wave to my favorite bodega owner, who gives me an extra orange each time I buy a bundle from him.

And as I walk, my mind wanders to the thing that's most been occupying it this last week: Smith Redfield.

I spent two more days at the summer house before I had to come home and work my shifts at summer camp and the restaurant. Which meant two whole days of being in his company, staring at him when he wasn't looking, and having actual conversations worthy of decent human beings.

He even let me have two strips of the bacon he cooked for breakfast the other day.

It's mortifying though, realizing that I harbor this girlish little crush on him. For starters, I used to date his best friend. Going after another guy in their friend group is just ... slutty. I know girls who do that, who hook up with their ex's friend just to get back at them. Or like the dynamic of that group, so they start sleeping around it. That's not me, and I've always found it kind of cheap.

Next, for all of the insults and tension he's thrown my way, I'd look like a complete idiot if I tried to throw myself at Smith. I have way more respect for myself than that, and I'm a stronger woman than one who goes after the sort of man who metaphorically pulls your pigtails on the playground.

But the biggest reason this infatuation with Smith Redfield

can go no further? He's made it extremely clear that he loathes me.

After picking up the lunch order I called into Fong's, my favorite Chinese place around the corner, I make my way back to my apartment.

I can practically smell the beef and broccoli as I climb the five flights of stairs, and my phone rings just as I'm about to pull my keys out.

"Hi, Dad," I say as I balance the bag of Chinese food on my hip so I can unlock my door.

"Hi, pumpkin. How you doing?" His raspy, cigarette-tinged voice comes through the phone.

My dad quit smoking nearly twenty years ago after a scare with lung cancer, but he still sounds like a sailor stumbling out of a hole-in-the-wall bar.

"Good, just got some Chinese for myself after taking a walk. Have to go to work a private party tonight."

"That's good tips, right there." I can picture Dad nodding through the phone.

He knows, because Mom has waited tables and worked catering jobs on the side for years.

"How are you? How's Mom?" I ask out of both curiosity and politeness.

Something clinks in the background, and I imagine he's in his truck. Even though it's Saturday, there are always jobs to be had. I can remember my dad missing on most weekends of my childhood because that meant overtime and off-hour pay.

"Oh, we're fine. Went to your cousin's daughter's christening the other day. Then I took your mom to bingo, she won a hundred dollars. So we sprang for a bottle of red wine."

"That sounds like such a nice weekend," I say as I set down my things in my tiny kitchen.

It's really just a pair of cabinets with a countertop, next to a small fridge and a stove.

"How was your week?" he asks.

My dad has always been a good one, he'll call and listen even if he doesn't entirely understand my life. During the Justin phase, he was the most stern he's ever been as my father. I was dating a banker who had no callouses on his hands, and Dad didn't know how to handle that.

"It was really good. Worked at summer camp and the restaurant, and at the beginning of the week I was at that summer house I rented with friends."

"Must be nice, being so fancy," Dad quips.

I know he isn't saying it to be nasty, but that's how I take it. Sometimes, my parents wear their blue-collar badge of honor too proudly. I appreciate everything they've done for me, and all they sacrificed to put me through college and support me growing up. It couldn't have been easy on a teacher and an electrician's salary, but they did it.

Except, sometimes I hate that they snub their noses at people who have higher salaries. Or those who buy nice homes, or wear expensive clothes. A lot of the time, those people worked really hard for their money, too.

When I told them I was doing the house share this summer, Mom nearly had a conniption, and went into hysterics that this wasn't the way they raised me. As if I'm not a school teacher, too, at a low-income district. As if I don't volunteer more time to help my kids after school. As if I don't wait tables to help pay my rent all on my own.

"Actually, it's been wonderful," I say, just to be spiteful.

"That's not what I meant, Molly." He sighs, and I know he regrets needling me. "I'm glad you're getting some time off. You work hard."

"You do, too, Dad. Isn't it time to bring on an apprentice?"

Dad is an electrician and has owned his own company since before I was born. He does pretty well, and he's known in our community as the guy to call if you have a problem. But he's too stubborn and is aging. His back is bad after so many years of manual labor, and he doesn't trust someone to come in and help him part-time, or possibly set someone up to buy the business and his clients. He's of the age that he could consider retiring, but I know he never will.

"*Phooey*. I don't need anyone running or stealing my business. I've done it all by myself, and that's how I'll continue to do it." His voice is defiant.

He'll be working until the day he collapses on a job site, and I worry about that. But it also keeps him busy, keeps his mind active, and so how can I argue with that?

"All right, Dad, well you just be careful. I'm going to go eat my food and then get ready for this event."

"Stay safe, pumpkin. Come visit if you get a spare day."

"I will," I say before hanging up, knowing I'll most likely spend that day in the Hamptons.

This summer is about me, and though I still may be breaking my back at two jobs, I'm going to take every free second I have to enjoy the well-earned vacation I invested in.

13

SMITH

Another sun drenched day turns into a firefly-lit night, and the whole summer house crew is congregating in the kitchen.

Peter and Marta are snacking on a cheese tray someone laid out, Ray is reading a book with his foot propped on one of the stools, Jacinda keeps running in and out trying outfits for the girls to decide on, Heather is mixing up some cocktails, and Molly is sitting on another stool sipping a glass of wine.

"Where are we going tonight?" Ray asks, looking up from some medical textbook.

"I was thinking we could head to Montauk again, check out the bar scene. I have a friend playing with his cover band, they do a lot of Kenny Chesney. Could be fun," Heather suggests.

Even though she wasn't friends with any of us, even less than Molly was though she was dating Justin, Heather has begun to fit in quite nicely. She's just as peppy as Marta, and she and Jacinda seem to bond over makeup and hair and that sort of shit. Peter finds her funny, and I have to admit that she's a pretty good cook.

"Why aren't you dressed?" Marta asks Molly.

"I think I'm going to stay in tonight, catch up on my shut eye. It's been a long week." She gives a sheepish smile.

"*No*, you can't! You have to come party with me, I've missed you!" Heather sticks out her lip in a pout.

Molly shrugs. "I'm tired, I'll just drag down your night. You go, have a blast, and then I'll come out tomorrow."

Heather pouts for one more second, but when she realizes it's not working, hugs her friend. "Fine. You better sleep, though. No working on lesson plans or actual work. I know you. Seriously, get some rest."

I sneak a glance at Molly, wondering how much down time she gives herself now that her friend pointed it out. God, she's beautiful. Every other girl in the room is dressed in heels and tight clothing, with makeup and all those manipulated thick curls down their back. But Molly is sitting on her stool in sweat shorts and a T-shirt, sunflower blond hair tucked behind her ears, and her bronzed skin free of any stitch of makeup. The only jewelry she wears is a tiny gold chain around her neck with an apple charm hanging off, and I bet it's because she's a teacher.

I wonder who gave it to her, and the thought that it might have been Justin makes my gut clench.

The group starts to rally, calling taxis and getting their last drinks before the bar in. Peter is on his way out when he taps my shoulder.

"Cab is here."

"Yeah, I'm going to stay back. Have some emails to catch up on. You have fun."

Peter walks off with a wave, but it's Marta who lingers behind, giving me a look. She hasn't said anything about me coming clean to Molly since the first night in the house, but I know she's been thinking it. I flip my middle finger up at her, just to remind her that I knew her when she had braces in fifth grade, and walk off into the house.

I do actually catch up on some emails, and every ten seconds it pops into my brain that I'm alone in the house with Molly, though I try to ignore it. About an hour later, I venture out to the big wraparound porch, keen on watching the waves slap the beach in the dark.

"Oh gosh!"

Molly's voice comes from the corner of the deck, and I can just barely make her out.

"Why are you sitting out here in the dark?" I ask.

"You scared me." As I move closer, I see she has one hand pressed to her chest, and the other is holding the stem of a wineglass. "I wanted to watch the ocean a while. It's peaceful out here when the house is empty."

Weird, we'd had the same thought.

"Mind if I join you?"

Her eyes meet mine, and even in the dark, I imagine the hazel irises widening in shock. "Uh, sure."

I take the rocker next to hers and try to dry swallow past the lump in my throat when I see her bare legs propped up on the railing in front of us. She looks so at peace, and I wish I could pick her up and set her in my lap, rocking us both in the same chair.

"Are you enjoying the summer?" I ask, trying my hardest to be nice.

It's not that I don't know how or that I can't strike up a conversation, but I've always been on one speed with this woman. Since the moment I knew she was off-limits, I put her in this category in my head, one where I needed to act like an asshole around her. Changing that behavior will be challenging, especially since in the few times I've done so, I've nearly blurted out that I'm in love with her. Or had it in my head that it would be a good idea to kiss her.

She looks over at me, though I keep my gaze forward. "I am. It's beautiful out here, and obviously the food and night life are just incredible. But I wasn't convinced I should even come after ..."

Molly breaks off, and we both know she's talking about the breakup.

"But I'm glad I did. It's been a great summer so far."

Something sticks in my brain, and I'm letting the thought out before I tell myself I shouldn't. "You haven't asked any of us if we've talked to him."

There is a tiny gasp, one she means to mask, but I catch it. "Who, Justin?"

"Yes," I say patiently, now that I'm on this train.

I can feel her shrug. "I know you're friends with him, and it's not my place."

"Typically, when a girl gets dumped, they want the details. I know for a fact you didn't get any closure, and yet you haven't nagged one of us to tell you how he's doing. If he's asked about you. I haven't even heard you complain about the guy who did you dirty, and I mean dirty. He's my friend, but what he did was beyond low."

Now I look at her, and those big hazel eyes are blinking right at me. "Uh ... I ... thanks? I never expected those words to come out of your mouth, to be honest."

I chuckle. "I can be nice."

"When you want to be," she quips back, and I'm impressed at how little she takes my shit anymore. "But I don't know. I don't want to talk about the breakup in the first place, since it was pretty awful for me. I felt blindsided. But I also don't think it's fair to put that on any of you. You didn't act the way Justin did, and you've all been friends for way longer than I was around. It wasn't my place to ask anyone to pick sides, or even tell me how he was doing."

"You're much more mature than I would be. I'd be fucking livid if a girl did that to me. And just so you know, that prick hasn't called me either since the day his plane took off."

I don't know why I'm revealing that information to her. Maybe it's because I'm also pissed at Justin, though not surprised. He'd seemed off for the month leading up to his big move, and now we all knew why. I just thought we were better friends than that, and especially after I lost Stephanie. How could a friend do that to his buddy who just went through a huge moment of grief?

Molly looks back out to the ocean.

"I should have seen it coming, that's the thing. As if his scheduled date nights and no deviations wasn't a red flag, the not being allowed to leave things at his apartment should have alerted the national guard. I was blind, but purposely so. Deep down, I knew there were so many suspicious things about how he handled our relationship, but I chose to ignore them. Because I loved him, I wanted to *be in love*. Justin felt like that guy, the one I could envision making a home with and creating a life with. So I willed it to happen, even though he was acting completely off my script."

The fact that she just admitted that she wanted Justin to be the guy she spent the rest of her life with ... it feels like she just plunged a knife right through the center of my chest.

Sometimes I wonder to myself how she doesn't see right through me. How I've managed to hide that I'm crazy in love with her. I know I've done a good job at being a total dickwad, but part of me doesn't understand how Molly doesn't realize that the guy who wants to spend his life with *her* is sitting just feet from her face.

"He's an idiot for letting you go."

The sentence hangs between us, and my heart hammers against my ribcage. I didn't mean for it to sound so ... romantic. But it did. And now I can't take it back, not that I'm scrambling to pull it out of the air and shove the words back down my throat. Maybe, like Marta said, it's time to take my shot.

"That's the nicest thing you've ever said to me," Molly whispers.

I shrug. "Must be the ocean breeze and the rocking chair. I let the jerk take a rest in my bed tonight."

I hear her swallow a sip of wine, and can feel the smile in her voice as she says, "Well, I'm not complaining. I kind of like this version of you."

14

MOLLY

I've never been a fan of birthdays.

Maybe it's because it just means we're getting older. Maybe it's because my parents could only ever afford to make me a Duncan Hines cake and blow up balloons in the basement while other kids were getting roller rink parties or taking their friends to the movies. Maybe it's because I find those who have "birthday months" to be completely exhausting.

But the main reason is just a lot simpler than any of those. I just don't love the attention. On your birthday, everyone wants to call it out, wants to ask you how shiny and new you feel on this day that's all about you. I've always been the type who wants a quiet dinner with a few friends, followed by my favorite slice of raspberry cheesecake from the bakery down the street from Aja. Then I like to watch one of my favorite movies, or cuddle up on a balcony with my favorite book.

Last year, I'd only been dating Justin for a couple of months when my birthday rolled around. He went all out, taking me to a fancy restaurant and bought me these diamond earrings that I've still never worn except for one or two of his work parties. They weren't me, and the whole thing was just so over the top. I remember lying in bed after he'd fallen asleep and feeling so low about my birthday.

That's how it always makes me feel, which is why I have no desire to celebrate it tonight in the Hamptons.

"We really don't have to do this" I whine, slumping down on my bed.

It's another session of getting ready with Heather, and per usual, she's attacked my face and hair until she's satisfied with the result. I have to admit, the smoky eyeshadow and the curls she spun into my hair make me look like a whole new woman, but I still don't like birthdays.

"We're going to a really nice, quiet restaurant. No clubbing or bars like you requested. And I even had your favorite cake shipped here. We're going." She gives me a stern look.

"It feels weird to have these people celebrating my birthday when ... well, they aren't really my friends."

I shrug and look at Heather in the mirror. She comes over and hugs me around my shoulders as we look at each other in the glass.

"You get to claim the couple friends now, because he's gone. And these people are your friends. You've spent nearly four weeks with them in this house, and I've seen you form bonds. They really like you, without that bag of dicks you used to date. They've never brought him up once, and I doubt the asshole has even called any of them to check in. You're a wonderful person, Mol, that's why I've been friends with you for so long. People want to be around you, and they want to celebrate you. You deserve this, so please don't sell yourself short."

"He hasn't called them. At least he hasn't called Smith," I tell her.

I haven't divulged to her the conversation we had on the porch a couple days ago. It's the nicest interaction that Smith and I have ever had, and something changed between us that night. I'm not sure why he even asked me how I felt about the breakup, but for the first time since I've known him, I feel like he genuinely cares about me. Even though a part of me wanted to tell Heather right away, it felt like my own little secret that I could giddily feast on for the last few days.

"How do you know that?" she asks, sliding silver hoops into her earlobes.

"He told me. The night you all went out but we stayed back, we actually had a nice conversation. And he told me that Justin was an idiot for letting me go."

I swear, Heather's mouth all but drops to the floor. "He said that? Grumpy asshole of the year said that? What in the—"

My smile, flirty and delicate, can't be contained. "I know. It was so strange."

I touch a finger to my lips, my mind drifting back to the way he looked at me on the porch.

"Wait a minute. You like him!" Her finger invades my daydream as she points it straight at me.

Brushing her off, I go to strap my sandals on. "I don't, I'm fresh off a breakup with his best friend. Plus, he hates my guts. It was just a nice thing to say."

Heather is eyeing me suspiciously. "I'm not fully buying it, but it's your birthday, so I'll let it rest. Now come on, we have to go or we'll miss our reservation."

She made a reservation at a place she knew I'd love, and I do. It's a fresh seafood restaurant, with chairs and tables in the sand and candles adorning almost every surface. The ambiance is beautiful, and the place is nice, but not overly fancy. They serve beer out of bottles and make you crack your own crab legs, and the whole meal is delicious.

And my best friend was right, in the end; sharing the night with our summer house share friends goes better than I ever thought it could. Peter and Jacinda buy me a book she knew I'd been eyeing, and Marta gifts me a bathing suit wrap from a boutique downtown that I'm sure was far too expensive. Heather presents me with a beautiful silver picture frame, with a black-and-white photo of us on the beach from the first week of summer.

And even though it's wonderful, I'm still in a funk with it being my birthday, especially since I had an idea about how this year would go. I thought when I turned thirty, I'd be making plans to get engaged or already be there. I thought this would be the year I'd be planning a wedding, or moving in with my boyfriend. It seemed like a big age jump, from the reckless twenties—not that I was ever reckless—to the mature, sophisticated thirties.

Instead, I'm single and spending the summer in an unfamiliar place, with unfamiliar people. So I excuse myself and head to the tiki bar that the restaurant features, just to get a moment to breathe.

I'm standing there as the bartender makes me a piña colada, because if you can't consume a drink of pure sugar and alcohol on your birthday, when can you, when Smith wanders up.

"You okay?" he asks, and it's as if he can read me at all times.

I smile up at him. "Fine. I'm just not the biggest fan of my birthday."

He drums his fingers on the bar. "I get that. I always had to be because my sister made it a big deal. I'm not sure what I'll do this year."

A wave of shock mixed with sadness passes over me. It's the first time he's ever mentioned his sister, and I don't want to say the wrong thing.

"I'm sorry, Smith. I know it will probably be very hard, but I think she'd want you to enjoy it." I hope that was sincere enough without stepping over the line.

Those blazing blue eyes stare directly at the ground, then

look up at me. When they do, there isn't any of the grief he just shared a moment ago.

"But this is about you. It's your birthday, you should be enjoying it."

Does he care whether or not I am? "I know. I just thought it would be ... different. I thought I'd be in a different place than where I am today. It sounds silly, but my birthday this year reminds me that I'm single. That sounds pathetic, but it does. I guess sometimes I think that I'm just not girlfriend or wife material."

An audible click rings out between us, and when I look at him, he's grinding his jaw as if he's trying to break a molar. But then his features clear, and he's back to this new Smith that I'm becoming quite smitten with.

"I didn't know if I should give this to you in front of everyone," he says, pulling something from the pocket of his linen summer pants.

Smith sets a small, black velvet jewelry box on top of the bar, and slides it the couple of inches over to me. I'm speechless, honestly, because I had no idea he even got me anything. I wouldn't expect him to, and the fact that there is a jewelry box sitting there has made my heart speed into a gallop worthy of the Kentucky Derby.

I'm honestly so shocked that I can't seem to reach out and take it.

"Open it." There is a grin that tinges his tone.

With shaky fingers, I retrieve the box and push open the lid. And gasp when I do.

Inside is a tiny gold wave charm, so delicate and beautiful that it brings a tear to my eye.

"I see you wear that apple necklace all the time, and I thought maybe you'd want to add to it. Remember your summer here."

It's a challenge to keep the tears out of my throat when I speak. "Smith, this is so beautiful. I ..."

"Just say thank you." He nods, his face unreadable.

And before I can say anything else, he backs away, looking at me for a few steps and then turning to walk back to our table. It's going to take me years to figure out what the hell just happened, and my head feels heavy with this latest development on the Smith Redfield front.

The night winds down with one last drink and two glorious pieces of cheesecake, and then I'm ready for bed. It's only when I'm sinking into the covers that I realize I have to pee, and venture out into the hallway.

And what would you know, I almost run smack dab into Smith. Again.

He catches me by the arms, just like last time, but there is no rude jab or chuckling smirk. No, the minute his hands are on my skin, something ignites between us.

Smith looks like a panther who has just caught his prey. "I have no idea why you think any man wouldn't kill to be with you. I just can't ..."

The hallway is dark, and I hear no sounds from anywhere. Smith is just staring at me, those lethal blue eyes making every nerve ending in my body go haywire. I can't seem to breathe or swallow, or even move my feet. He's unreadable, so much intensity in his expression that I can't decipher.

And just when I think he's about to turn around and go back into his bedroom, he closes the foot of space between us—to capture my lips in the most searing, soul-crushing kiss I've ever experienced.

15

SMITH

Molly was standing there in our shared hallway, and I just couldn't help myself anymore.

After her birthday dinner, with her in that burnt orange dress that was cut so low in the back, I physically had to restrain myself from touching her skin as she climbed into the cab. And before that, when I'd given her the charm, that tender look on her face as if I was the only man who'd ever truly seen her.

I don't know what possessed me to buy her that gift. It's such an outright display of affection, when I've barely had two nice conversations with her. Getting her that charm all but exposes my feelings for her, and I saw Molly look at me with different shades in those hazel eyes when she'd opened it. I'd seen the charm in a jewelry store around the block from the new restaurant location and knew immediately I had to buy it for her. I'd had no intention of giving it to her, not really, but then Jacinda mentioned her birthday dinner and …

My vision had gone red with fury when she'd been at the bar, by herself, on her birthday, lamenting about how men just didn't want to make her a longtime option. Couldn't she see that I was desperate to hang onto her forever?

Fate certainly intervened when she stepped out of her room at the exact same time I was heading for our shared bathroom. Again, caught in an uncompromising position, there was no way I was squandering this softball from the heavens once again.

And now I'm holding her, really wrapping my arms around her, as my tongue invades her mouth.

This isn't the kiss of a guy looking to get laid, or of one who saw an easy target and went for it. This isn't the kiss of two people who want to use each other to get off, or the kiss of two people grieving the end of something in their own personal lives and seeking satisfaction.

This was the kiss of a man who had waited for more than three hundred and sixty-five days to take this woman's mouth. This was a kiss with all of the emotions and passion I'd been locking away inside my heart while she fell in love with my best friend. This was the kiss of a starving person, one who thought they'd never get this chance, and one who was pouring everything into it because he may never get this chance again.

"Smith," Molly moans my name into my mouth, and I could die a happy man from that sound alone.

I nip at her bottom lip, suckling the plump, full skin there. She tastes like the piña colada she had at dinner, and I want to drown in her. At first, it was just my intensity, driving at her full force as my mouth plied and explored hers. But now, Molly is matching me kiss for kiss. Her fingers have wound their way into my hair, and it feels like eons ago that I pinned her back to the wall and starting fucking her mouth with my tongue.

If I only get this one chance, I'm doing it right. So I throw everything I have at her; gentle kisses, hard ones, biting at the corners of her mouth, sucking her tongue into my own. My hands find their way under her shirt, and I stroke the velvet skin at her hips. My cock is so hard, I wouldn't be surprised if it leaves a bruise on her stomach, where it's wedged between us. She's so small, so short in comparison to me, that I'm practically pulling her up to my mouth.

The sounds she's making, Jesus fuck, I'm never going to be able to forget them. I'm not even inside her and this is the single most thrilling sexual moment I've ever had.

I'm about to move my hands higher, my balls tingling in anticipation of getting my hands on her perfect set of tits. I'm so giddy and drunk on arousal that I'm practically humping her in the hallway, but I've held this at bay for more than a year. Now that I've let myself fully off the leash, I'm not sure I can go back on it.

But the click of a door opening somewhere in the house breaks the spell, and Molly suddenly wrenches her head back, a soft thud sounding in the dark as her head connects with the wall.

Those murky green and amber eyes are so drunk with lust but saucer wide at the same time, I know I've completely befuddled her. There is a harsh, stinging ache in my chest and I want desperately to haul her against me and carry her to my bed as she straddles my waist.

I can't do it, though. She doesn't know, has no clue what this would mean to me. And from her words at dinner, she'll think I'm just another one of those guys who doesn't see her as anything other than a temporary now.

So I plant one more lingering kiss on her forehead and fade back into my room, as much as it physically hurts to leave her in the hallway.

I come in my boxers on a silent curse, my other hand gripping the edge of my nightstand, as I think about what it will feel like when I eventually do get Molly naked, beneath me, completely open to the idea of us.

16

SMITH

The next morning, I'm sitting at the kitchen island as the housemates wake up and come in one by one.

I threw on a bathing suit before coming in, and the coffee I'm drinking tastes extra sweet this morning. In fact, everything seems brighter. My head is clearer. I was up before dawn, just lying in the tangled sheets, thinking about Molly's taste that was still on my mouth.

"Morning," Peter grumbles, his hair a sleep-tossed mess and his eyes half open.

Marta and Ray trail behind him, also in beach gear, and she goes to the cabinet and pulls down a box of cereal.

"Make me a bowl?" I give her a begging look.

"Do you do any of the cooking around here?" She rolls her eyes. "You would never know you're in the restaurant business."

"Hey, I just run the joint. I can't cut a pepper or stir a pot to save my life." I hold up my hands in faux surrender.

She begrudgingly pours out a third bowl, and then practically tosses it across the counter. "Thanks, Marty."

"Don't call me that," she warns, pointing a threatening finger in my direction.

"Why are you so chipper this morning?" Peter finally speaks after about five minutes and ten sips of coffee.

I shrug, and at that moment, Molly makes her entrance. Her long blond locks are braided down her back, and she's wearing a simple lilac sundress that floats around her. Her lean, strong arms are bare, and I can't help but stare at her lips as she walks to the coffee pot, purposely avoiding my gaze.

"I just had a nice night last night," I say, hoping she catches my drift in this room full of people.

"It was a great night, I hope you had such a good birthday!" Jacinda goes up to hug Molly from behind.

A laugh comes from Molly, who hugs Jacinda back. It's nice to see that the rest of the house is finally forming some solid friendships with her, and that she's opened herself up to the possibility. We've been here for a month, almost, and it's as if she was never just the girlfriend of one of our friends. Molly has established herself in the group, and the sting of Justin's betrayal is fading by the day.

"I did. It was one of the best birthdays I've ever had, actually." She smiles at everyone but me.

"The big three oh, huh? What're you gonna do in this decade?" Ray asks her politely.

Molly shrugs, pulling her toast out of the toaster and smearing some peanut butter on it. "Honestly? The same thing I have been doing?"

We all chuckle a little, and I try to catch her eye, but she's still not looking at me. Everyone goes about their breakfast, remaining pretty much quiet, and at some point, Jacinda and Marta go out on the porch.

"Hey, Smith, can you help me get the packages from out front?" Molly finally addresses me, but her voice sounds too anxious.

Marta looks between us, though she seems to be the only one who notices the strange interaction.

"Sure," I say, almost chuckling under my breath.

So, she's freaking out about this. Hm, not the route I thought she'd automatically take, but I'm not surprised. With the way I kissed her, after giving her that birthday present, she was probably so fucked-up in the head about me, she couldn't see straight.

I follow her out to the front and see only two tiny Amazon packages sitting on the porch. "This is what you needed help with?"

She folds her arms over her chest, leveling me with a scolding stare. "No, and you know that. We have to talk about last night."

"What about it?" I shoot her a sly grin, and my gaze falls on her lips.

"Stop that," she hisses.

"Why? Because we're alone out here and I can think of only one thing I want to do." I advance a little on her.

She backs up, looking startled.

"Why are you flirting with me? I don't get it, you hate me." Molly sounds dumfounded.

I have to chuckle, because it's so far from what I feel about her. "If only that were the case."

"Smith, you have tormented me and belittled me for an entire year. I'm not even sure you know a decent thing about me." She guffaws, as if I've just told her that I'm related to the Queen of England.

That burns me, probably because it's true. And I'm the one who has perpetrated this narrative, the one where I think so little of her and her lifestyle. I've managed to convince her that she's nothing in my eyes, and I wish I could punch myself in the face at this moment.

Using my body, I corner her, our faces so close that I can smell the sweet mint on her lips.

"I know that you're a fifth grade teacher, and that you do so much more than teach. You volunteer at their after-school program three times a week, so they don't have to go home to empty kitchens. And that's before you take a restaurant shift to make more money to give those kids more. I know that you didn't have the easiest childhood, and that you hate carrots in your soup. When we went bowling that one time, you whooped our asses, even though Justin made you feel awkward for doing so. I wanted to deck him that night. You prefer candy over popcorn at the movies and stop on the street to give the homeless whatever spare money you have in your wallet. Do you know how many people just pass them by? I know that you put up with Justin's obnoxious mother for an entire Saturday just to learn how to make his favorite pot roast, and that you re-read your favorite novels because it transports you to a world, even for a few hours, where you don't have to rely on only yourself for everything. And I know that I—"

I break off, almost blurting out that I'm in love with her. That I want to be the one she does all of those things with, or for. But I clam up. I've already said enough.

"Ho-How do you know all that?" Her voice is a hair's breadth above a whisper, and she looks shocked, as if she's just seen an actual ghost.

"Because I've listened to you for the last three hundred and sixty-five odd days. Every time you spoke, I digested that small piece of information as if it was food and I was a starving man. I want to know everything about you, Molly. But you were with my best friend. What was I supposed to do?"

I'm really asking the question, because I want to know her answer now. Justin isn't here, and though bro code still might be in effect, I'm saying fuck it. If she could want me like she wanted him, or even half as much, I'd take it. I'm that desperate.

Molly squares her chin at me and proves that she's much more defiant than she's acted toward me in the time she was with Justin.

"You should have been kind and built a relationship with me as a friend. Not pushed me away and thrown barbs at me every other sentence like some envious coward. If you're even being truthful."

A sense of dread fills my chest, because I may have fucked this up beyond my control.

"Molly, I—" I go to reach for her, plead my case, but she swats me away and walks to the other side of the porch.

"No, Smith. I need ... I need to think. You spun my entire world on its axis last night. Seriously, everything I believed about you turned out to be the opposite and now you're telling me this? Can't you understand why I would be confused?"

I gulp, trying to get ahold of myself, and think like a rational human being. "Yes, yes. I can understand that."

Backing off, I give her some space, and run my fingers through my hair. "I've waited a year, I can wait for you to wrap your head around this."

Molly hunches over a little, an absurd laugh breaking free of her throat. "This is the strangest revelation I've ever had."

"I could kiss you again. Maybe it would make it clearer?" I switch back to my flirty, seductive voice.

"Get out of here." She rolls her eyes before walking back inside, leaving me on the porch with the packages.

17

SMITH

"There is no way in hell I'm letting you buy glassware that looks like this. Steph would roll over in her grave."

My brother's words make me both cringe and want to smack him. Not only is he making fun of the glasses that Campbell and I picked out for the new restaurant, but he's trying to make jokes about our sister's death.

"Too soon." I cut him a look that says I'm not taking his shit today.

"Touchy, touchy. Fine, baby bro, I'll stop with the lightheartedness, but I swear, if you buy these highballs, I will never eat at this restaurant."

He scrunches his nose up and places the glass back on the shelf. When Harrison, my oldest brother, said he'd accompany me to the restaurant depot to start selecting things for the new restaurant, I hesitated. He's an awesome interior designer, but there is a reason I don't hire him on my projects. We butt heads way too much, and his taste is much more elegant than the rustic charm I'm going for at Stefania.

But I trust his judgment, and he's been nagging me the entire summer to have a brother's trip, so I brought him along.

Harrison is the oldest boy, but second kid, in our family. It goes Katrina, Harrison, Juliette, Gianna, Stephanie and me, Burton, and then Erica is the baby. We're all separated by a year or two, and Harrison is six years older than I am. So, since I was about nine years old, I've known that my oldest brother is gay. It's a normal thing in our house, nothing that my parents freaked out over, and I'd like to think our family took it in stride.

Plus, Harrison's husband, Kenneth, is now Mom's favorite child, and he isn't even blood. Kenneth is a florist and brings her fresh roses every week. He always gets the best piece of spaghetti pie for Christmas, is the first to be served at any family dinner, and she waits on him hand and foot.

We walk down the aisles of the depot together, brainstorming about the right color scheme and plate shape. Everything down to the tongs on the forks at a restaurant has to be perfect, has to be on brand. Sometimes, even the most minute of details can make or break a place.

"Ma is trying to start the plans for the memorial," Harrison tells me, shoving aside a glass he doesn't like.

I grunt, some indiscernible noise, hoping he drops this subject.

Of course, he doesn't. "You need to think about what you'll say. Everyone will expect you to give the 'keynote' speech, and you know it."

With the way he's looking at me, I know he's insinuating something about the funeral. When we buried my twin sister a little over seven months ago, I could barely even stand to be in the church. My whole family was grieving, but for me, it was the worst.

No wonder, Stephanie and I had grown together since the minute we were a blip on a screen. She was my partner in crime, from the moment we entered the world to the minute she left it. We had the kind of freaky connection that books and movies always describe. I could literally tell what she was thinking, and she could feel it when I was injured, even if she was hours away from me.

My parents had asked if I could give the eulogy, and I shot them down immediately. I should have been stronger for Steph, should have swallowed my grief for the day and gotten up in front of our family and told them the best parts about my sister. But I couldn't. I felt like I was drowning, still do some days, and now Harrison is all but confirming that our mother wants me to give the speech at her memorial this winter. The one-year anniversary of her death.

When I got that call the days after New Year's, I thought that my little sister Erica had been joking. But no, our little sister frantically dialed my number when the paramedics rushed Steph into the emergency room she worked at as a nurse. Car accident, hit straight on by a drunk driver in a tractor trailer. Steph was barely conscious when they pulled her body from the driver's seat, and she surrendered to her injuries just minutes after the hospital staff began life saving procedures. In essence, she never had a chance. She was thirty-one years old.

Later, we'd find out that the guy driving the truck had been loaded, blowing a .18 blood alcohol level when the cops caught him trying to flee the scene of the accident. He was high on something too, some kind of prescription pill that I can never remember. We all had to go to court, watch him get sentenced to ten years in prison with the possibility of parole in a just a few short years. A decade, probably less with overcrowding, for murdering my twin sister.

The thought still makes me want to shatter every breakable item in this restaurant depot. I've gotten counseling, tried the stages of grief, and nothing has helped yet. I want to strangle the guy who killed her with my bare hands, until I see the light go out of his eyes.

"I'm not giving a speech," I say tersely, trying to shut down this conversation.

"Smith, I know it's horrible. I never thought we'd be coming up on a year without her, either. But we need to remember the good times. You need to keep her memory alive."

Every word he says is like a dagger in my heart. "You don't understand."

"Don't tell me I don't understand. I lost my sister, too." Harrison's voice is dangerously close to the edge of anger.

"You don't!" I explode, garnering the attention of other shoppers. "She might have been your sister, but she was a *part of me*. We shared the same womb. The day she died, it was like a part of me died, too. You will never understand how that feels."

His eyes, the same color as mine, ignite with rage. "You have to get over your own anger about her death and grow the fuck up. Our family needs you, we all need to ban together in this. Mom hates that she can't talk to you about this, that we can't even touch the subject when you're in the room. We're all hurting. We know you're hurting most, but we're your family. If you let this fester, it's going to infect your whole life. As it is, you hole up with work or alone most days of the week. I haven't seen you truly happy since months before Steph even died, and you haven't given any woman a chance in forever. I don't want to see this for you, Smith."

"Fuck you. Fuck you for saying that." I growl at him, the spiteful, rage-filled monster clawing to make its way out of my chest.

I can't even look at Harrison right now, and don't know how this whole shopping trip went sideways so quickly. Leaving my cart in the middle of the aisle, I storm out of the store, not even waiting for my brother. He met me here in his car, so I stomp to mine, getting in and peeling out of the parking lot.

It's immature, not facing the discussion and reacting the way I did, but I'm not ready. My family seems to have moved into the sad but bittersweet mourning period, where they can all sit around and talk about Steph with fondness. I can't do that.

It's been two days since I saw Molly, and even though I told her I'd give her some space, my argument with Harrison has me jonesing for the one good thing I can do.

Which is to be in her presence.

Pulling out my cell phone, I call the one sibling of mine who I know will give me no grief, will just listen, or go along with what I need.

When she picks up, I ask, "Gi, can I take you to dinner?"

18

MOLLY

It's been four days since Smith kissed me in the hallway.

No, not kissed. That's too mild of a word for what he did to me. Turned my world upside down, maybe? Pulled a blindfold off my heart? I think that the term obliterated might be the best one to describe this situation.

Smith Redfield obliterated my initial impression of him. He obliterated my idea of what a good kiss was. And my brain? It feels completely obliterated with this idea that Smith has ... what? Liked me since the moment he saw me?

He said a year. That for the entire year or so that Justin and I were together, he hung on every factoid I gave him.

I feel like everything I thought I knew has been flipped upside down, and I don't know how to process it. Sure, in the last few weeks it's been difficult to ignore the growing crush I have on Smith. Honestly, I've always been attracted to him in a physical sense, even when I was with his best friend. You'd have to have no pulse to ignore the beauty of that Italian demigod.

But with the way he's treated me, I ... it's hard to push past that. For an entire year, I thought the man hated me. I had this bitterness in my mind whenever I had to deal with him and felt so insecure and intimidated. I hate that I felt that way around a man.

So, I've had four days to think about it, really three since I confronted him on the porch. The next day, I left to come back for the city and summer camp, and so I've had two whole Smith-free days to really consider how I feel about all of this.

Obviously, that kiss was ...

Stupendous. Jaw-dropping. The best kiss, let alone sex, I've ever had, and we weren't even naked. If that's how the man kisses, I can only imagine the things he'll make me feel in bed.

But it was more than that. I've had this stupid, girlish attraction to Smith for a while, but never paid it more mind. He couldn't possibly feel anything for me, so why dwell? That's what I had thought. Then, before he even admitted to watching me the entire year I was with Justin, he kissed me and it changed something in my brain.

The feelings I have for Smith now are more than just a surface-level crush. I can't explain it, but the way in which he adored my mouth, poured his emotions out without so much as a word ... a switch flipped in me. I looked at him differently, and the way my heart rate increased when I thought about him now isn't the same as an innocent flirtation.

I could really see something happening between us.

And a month fresh off a breakup with a guy I thought I'd marry ... I was terrified of feeling that.

"I just seated a couple in your section, they requested you." Maria, the hostess at Aja, hustles by me with menus in her hands.

It's another Thursday night at the restaurant, and we've been swamped with diners. My feet are killing me, even in my ugly but comfortable black sneakers, and I'm starting to develop a pounding in my temples. Most nights, I don't mind being a waitress; it's great money, and the conversation is usually interesting with a couple of tables. But tonight, I'm not feeling it at all.

"Thanks," I tell Maria as I pick up drinks from the bar to deliver to another one of my tables.

After checking on my tables and making sure they don't need anything, I swoop around to the new couple.

And stop short when I spot who it is.

A busboy nearly slams into my back, and I apologize profusely, turning heads, including his.

My feet are wobbly as they walk up to the table where Smith sits opposite a gorgeous blond woman who looks like she's just come out of the courtroom arguing a case. Her sleek white skirt suit is one of those expensive, fashionable ones, the kind you wear a silk night shirt underneath and still manage to make it look professional. Which she is. Her features are fox-like, and she's the kind of woman you stare at without realizing you're even doing it.

The twisting knots of jealousy in my stomach make me want to both flee into the kitchen, and slap him in the face. He kissed my socks off only four days ago, and now he has the balls to show up at my job and flaunt a date in my face? Is this his idea of giving me space? I told him to basically stop with the immature bullshit, because he should have copped to having feelings for me a long time ago, and this is his plan to ... what? Woo me?

It kills me that it's kind of working, because I wouldn't be surprised to see my cheeks twenty shades of green right now.

"Molly, what a pleasant surprise," Smith says, a devious twinkle in his eye.

As if he didn't know I worked here, or that I most likely had a shift each night I wasn't in the Hamptons.

I have to swallow the rude retort and put on my best you're-an-asshole-but-I-want-a-good-tip face. "Smith, thank you for dining with us tonight. What can I start you two off with? We have a wonderful cabernet bottle we're featuring tonight, or perhaps a bottle of champagne. We should start your date night off right."

My tone has so much bitterness during that last sentence, and I can't even contain it. My professional mask is slipping by the second, but Smith has just added the straw that's breaking the camel's back on this whole crappy night.

His blond dream girl snickers into her napkin, and Smith looks like I've just poured a drink in his lap.

Neither of them answers me, so I push forward. "You know what, I'll just give you two another moment to decide."

Because I can't stand in front of them any longer. I stride off, my heart burning with embarrassment and the urge to cry pressing at the corner of my eyeballs.

"Molly." I can hear Smith coming after me, following me, and I swerve through the dining room into a dark back corner.

"I can't believe I fell for that crap on the porch." I get all up in his face. "It was just another one of your mean pranks, wasn't it? Fool me into thinking you felt something for me, just so you could see my face when you did this? You're a piece of shit, honestly, Smith. Why can't you just leave me—"

"She's my sister. Her name is Gianna," he explains, and by the look on his face, I know he's telling the truth.

Oh. Well, *crap*.

"You … you don't look anything alike." I sneak a glance at her from the hallway containing the point-of-sale computer and extra wineglasses.

"That's what Botox and hair dye will do, but don't tell her I said that. I also am not telling you that she's shaved her unibrow since the fourth grade." He smirks like a little boy tattling on his sibling.

Smith tells me this to try to make me smile, but I'm too

jacked up on the adrenaline of my diatribe that I only got to half spew.

"Well, why are you even here? You knew I was working, so you wanted me to wait on you?" That idea stings even more than him coming here on a date with another woman.

Smith drops his head to his chest, rubbing a hand over his forehead. "I can see now that my plan really was not thought out. I should have just asked to come over to your apartment, cooked you dinner or brought you flowers. I just ... I wanted to see you. I thought this might be a good way."

And my heart is a mushy puddle by my feet. Surly, brooding Smith is insanely attractive, but Smith being sweet? That's just downright irresistible.

My attitude softens, and part of me wants to walk into him and get a great big hug, but I refrain. "Sorry, it's just been a really long night. I'm ... I'm actually kind of glad to see you."

"Miss me?" he asks, grinning like a fool.

"I didn't say that." My smile is shy. "Go back to your sister, I'll grab you that bottle of cabernet, it's good."

"That would be great. I really want you to come meet her. She'll think it's hilarious you accused her of being my date."

My cheeks burn. "Oh God, that's going to be embarrassing."

He reaches out, stroking my cheek with one finger. "No, it won't be. I'll make sure of it."

We stand there for a moment, his hand lingering on my face, and I just blink up into his eyes. What the heck is happening between us?

Smith goes back to his table, and I fetch the bottle of red wine. I bring it back, uncorking it for them, and spend a few minutes being introduced to Gianna, who is a high-powered lawyer in the city. She's brilliant and beautiful, but down to earth and doesn't look at me through privileged lenses. I'm pleasantly surprised, to use Smith's words, that the whole meal is quite nice. It doesn't feel like I'm waiting on them, and they're both so warm and inviting that I end up talking to them a lot about their family growing up.

When it comes time for the bill, I drop it by Smith, and tell him not to worry about the tip. "Please, it will make me feel weird."

He raises an eyebrow at me. "Fine, but you have to agree to something else, then."

"And what's that?" I smile, directing it to Gianna who looks at her brother in anticipation.

"A date. With me. This weekend." It's like he's daring me.

My heart flutters, and my throat goes dry. He's given me as much space as his ego will allow, I suppose. And the time he's been in the restaurant tonight has been the bright spot of my shift.

I take a deep breath, knowing I'm about to stumble into something unknown. "Okay. I will."

19

MOLLY

I still can't believe I agreed to go on a date with Smith Redfield.

My brain still feels like it's been thrown for a literal loop, but here I am, waiting out front of our summer house in pretty white linen shorts and a chambray tank top, waiting for Smith to meet me out here.

It's only Ray at home right now, and even if he saw us leaving together, we could say that we were just getting groceries or liquor. But I came out here alone because I'm not sure if Smith wants anyone to know what we're doing. I'm shocked he even asked me, or that he likes me at all in the first place.

Likes me sounds like such a juvenile phrase, but I can't think of a better one. And that's what this is, right? He's admitting he had a crush on me when I was dating Justin, isn't that what he meant?

Either way, there are butterflies in my stomach the size of eagles. My hands are sweating, which is gross but true, and I can't stop nervously shifting from foot to foot.

"Hey, sorry. Just had to grab my wallet." Smith comes down the front porch steps, and my mouth goes dry.

Does he have to be this gorgeous? As if it's not already an unfair advantage going on a date with him, what with his charm, professional success and overall intimidating personality. No, to top it all off, the man has to look like he could be a character in the next Marvel movie.

His jet-black hair is gelled to the side, in that suave European sort of way that also makes his jawbone look impossibly cut. In a hunter green T-shirt that clings to his pecs, biceps, and abs, and white shorts that highlight the strain of his thighs when he walks, it will be a miracle if I survive this date with dry underwear.

"That's okay, I just thought I'd wait out here."

I also needed a moment to collect myself. This will be the first date I've been on in more than a year, and it isn't just some throwaway. This isn't a setup by Heather or some half-cocked dating app meetup that I could shrug off if it didn't go well. The ramifications of this date, this man, loom so much larger. If this doesn't work out, we still have to share a summer house together. If this doesn't work out, I will still have to sleep in the room next to Smith for the next month, and see him at functions for years to come if these people decide to keep me as a friend after the summer ends.

Plus, this feels *bigger* in my heart. You know that sense of largeness you get, that you can't put words to? Like the universe is aligning or something? That's how I feel right now. I am on the verge of jumping into something after I've barely recovered from getting my heart broken.

"I called us a cab, in case we want to have a drink or something. Plus, I doubted you wanted to take the bike out the first time we went somewhere together," Smith says, right as an Uber pulls down the driveway.

Nodding, I let him open the door of the Uber for me. "And you'd be correct. Not to mention, it freaks me out a little."

Smith rounds the car, a grin on his face. When he slides in on the other side, he says, "Oh, I'll get you on that bike. But I'll give you a pass tonight."

I clench the muscles in my core, because the way he just said he'll get me on the bike. Well, it sounds like he'd like to put something entirely different between my legs. And now I'm blushing. *Hard.*

The sun is setting as we drive through the Hamptons; the trees swaying in the midsummer breeze. People pedal colorful pastel bikes along the road, and every once in a while, we pass a roadside restaurant where patrons spill onto outdoor picnic tables.

"Where are we going?" I ask to break up the silence.

"Well, I figured we both spend a lot of time in restaurants, so I thought we'd do something different."

"Okay?" I can't help the curious grin that sneaks out.

He took the time to think about my daily schedule, and to be honest, I'm not a huge fan of sit-down meals. Yes, I want to have a conversation with Smith, desperately do, but I see enough people sit through hours long meals per week. I'd rather stretch my bones.

The Uber driver swings into a parking lot, and a fake waterfall catches my attention.

"No way." I start to laugh. "You're taking me mini-golfing?"

"We wouldn't be at the beach if we didn't mini-golf, right?" Smith's smirk is dazzling. "Don't move."

He bolts out of the car and jogs around to open my door, taking my hand. The minute our fingers touch, a zing of electricity goes from the tips of my fingers to my toes.

After he signs us in at the stand with a bored-looking teenage girl, we pick out our clubs and then our balls.

"Red, huh?" I say, observing his choice.

"Like Tiger on Sundays." He winks. "And you, yellow?"

"My favorite color, like the sunset," I tell him.

"Loser has to buy ice cream." Smith lets me walk ahead of him onto the green for the first hole, which is around a clapping plastic dolphin and some starfish.

We shoot our first shots, and I come closer to the hole than he does. Which sounds dirty, and I immediately think so, but have to bite my lip to keep from laughing. Or gloating.

"Do you play golf often?" I ask, trying to make conversation.

After lining up his shot and sinking it in on the second try, Smith looks at me. And when he looks at me, I feel like he's looking right through my clothes.

"No, not really. I'm usually working. And, well, I typically only ever work. And if I'm not truly working, I'm at the restaurant, wondering what else I can do to work more."

I chuckle. "Wow, and here I thought you had a wild social life."

"Mostly just overseeing the businesses, to be honest. Is that what happens when you love your job? God, I sound like all those people I used to make fun of when I was a kid and wanted to be Bear Grylls when I grew up." We move onto the next hole, quickly going through that one and then onto the third.

"No, I know what you mean. It's only halfway through the summer and I'm already developing lesson plans in my head. Thinking about what I can do to engage my students this year. If I could work round the clock to improve their lives, I would. So I get it. I'd always rather be teaching."

Smith asks me more questions about my class, my school and some other surface level topics as we move through the course. We talk about his new restaurant and the vibe he's trying to give it; I tell him a little about my mom and dad, and we laugh about sharing the same hatred for laugh-track comedy shows.

"So, we're on a date," I say stupidly after a lapse in conversation, immediately wanting to kick myself.

"We are." He grins.

"Do you think the other housemates know?" I ask, thinking this whole thing is funny.

Smith's midnight blue eyes go cloudy. "Only if you told Heather. I didn't tell anyone else. I thought we could just enjoy tonight, ourselves."

My heart stutters, because the way he said that doesn't sound encouraging.

"Let's not tell anyone in the house," Smith says, his eyes shifting around.

My stomach plummets, dropping in that nauseous way it does right before you're hurtled over the edge of the roller coaster drop. "Yeah, that makes sense."

I turn away, pretending to line up my shot so I can chew on my lip and try not to let him see the shame burning at the corner of my eyes. It shouldn't be a surprise that Smith wants to keep us a secret, but it still guts me. It's the same feeling I had the first time I told Luke Evans that I liked him in the sixth grade, and he showed the note to the entire class and then completely turned me down. That sick-to-your-stomach, want-to-go-home-and-cry-into-your-pillow feeling invades my throat, and I completely bungle my shot on this sixteenth hole.

It's Smith's turn, and I walk past him without saying a word or looking at him. I can't. Not now, not when I know he wants to keep me a secret. The icky slime of that realization sits heavy on my heart as he takes his next shot. You could hear crickets as we walk down the hole, the infamous windmill shot tripping me up epically on the first, second, and third tries.

I get so frustrated, from my ball being spit back out, that I make a tiny whimpering noise. But it's just a facade for the real problem—Smith wanting to keep this date a secret. Keep me a secret.

"Hey, you okay?" He reaches for my arm, turning me to him.

I avoid his eye and bite my lip to keep the tears at bay. "Fine."

Smith sighs. "I'm no expert on women, but even I know that means you're so far from fine. I grew up with sisters, remember? What did I do wrong?"

I feel like a sullen child as I try to speak through the lump in my throat. "You ... do you not want to tell the house because you're embarrassed to be on a date with me?"

One second I'm separated from him, and the next, strong arms are pulling me in, and two fingers tilt under my chin so that I have to look him in the eyes. When I do, they're fierce and intense upon mine.

"Don't even think that. Not for one second. I'm an idiot, Molly. I didn't mean it in that way, by no means am I embarrassed by you. Hell, if anyone is out of their league on this date, it's me. I seriously don't deserve to have an ounce of your attention. I just said that because, well, you were with Justin. I don't know how weird my friends would be with me dating my best friend's ex, plus we're roommates so that complicates things. And I just want some time for us. I don't want to share our connection with other people, or invite their criticism or opinions on us dating. For a little while, I just want to stay in the bubble with you. Can we have our bubble, even if for just a moment?"

In the back of my mind, my brain doubts what he's saying. But with the way Smith is looking at me, my heart can't help but be convinced. Hopefully, I won't get burned, but I don't think I could stop now even if I knew that would be the outcome.

We finish up our round of golf, and I end up beating him, though I think he might have bungled his last shot on purpose. I get a hot-fudge dipped cone and Smith gets a mint chocolate chip milkshake from an ice cream shop two storefronts down from the mini-golf place, and then we head back to the house.

About an hour later, I'm getting ready for bed, our date kind of ending in a parting of ways because the other housemates had already arrived home. I won't say I wasn't disappointed that Smith didn't sneak in a little kiss on the porch, but it was probably too risky.

The door is open as I turn the faucet on, prepping it for hot water to wash my face. I pull my toothbrush from the over-the-sink mirror cabinet, and squirt some toothpaste on it. Just as I'm about to put it in my mouth, Smith comes in, standing behind me with a wry smirk on his face. I can't help the shy smile that spreads over my lips as we stare at each other in the mirror.

He reaches past me, to open the mirror and grab his own toothbrush, then repeats the process I did.

We stand there, brushing our teeth together, and it's so normal that it feels hilarious. But at the same time, it's a moment that's bringing us closer together. I've always wanted to be with a man who will participate in the most mundane of activities with me, but do so just because he wants to be near me. That's what Smith is doing right now, and my heart is practically melting.

After a minute or two of eye-flirting in the mirror while we brush, I try to daintily spit and wash off my toothbrush. Without thinking, I set my brush down and back up, wondering if I should leave.

"Did you just leave your toothbrush on the sink?" Smith says through a gob of toothpaste in his mouth.

"Maybe I did." I shrug one shoulder flirtily.

He spits his out, wipes the back of his mouth with his hand, and then comes toward me. Any shred of disappointment left from the anticlimactic end of our date is wiped away.

Because he slides his palms to my cheeks, blinks once, and gives me the best first date kiss I've ever gotten.

20

SMITH

This is going to be an awful day.

I can just tell, from the moment I wake up, that grief is shrouding me like a cloud that won't lift. It happens sometimes, ever since Stephanie passed. My eyes will open in the morning, and I just know that the reality of her death is going to sit more heavily on me that day than it does some others.

When I go to lift myself out of bed, my limbs feel like gelatin, and my temples are pounding as I pull on a fresh pair of boxers. As I'm pissing and brushing my teeth, a zing of fury so palpable rushes up my spine, that I have to hold myself back from punching the mirror above the sink.

There is only one thing to do, and thank God I'm in the Hamptons so I can go to a place that might help.

As soon as I step out of my room in a T-shirt and athletic shorts, Molly is crossing the hall to the bathroom. She's wearing tight workout pants and a tank top, and even with the state of my mood, my cock perks up at the sight of her curves.

"Morning. Where are you off to?" she asks with a smile, spotting my backpack and water bottle.

"Shadmoor State Park." My voice is curt and gruff.

"Oh ... okay." Her smile instantly vanishes, and I know she thinks she's done something wrong.

"It's not about you, Molly." The words out of my mouth make this even worse.

And her face completely shutters. "Right. Of course."

She's about to shuffle off awkwardly to the bathroom, and I gently grab her elbow. Sighing through gritted teeth, I try to keep my grief and mourning at bay for a moment.

"I had a great time last night, this isn't about that. I'm just ... I need to go somewhere. Get out of your head, you didn't cause this. It's just ... I have to go out."

Still, even with my explanation, I can see her visibly shrinking in front of me. I've done this, caused her to think this way. After a year of speaking to her with little more than veiled disdain, of course she thinks my reaction this morning has something to do with rejecting her.

Molly is about to speak, to pull herself away and try to hide her emotional response when I talk first.

"Come with me?"

The question pops out before I can stop it, and once it's out, I want to take it back. I wanted to go on the hike alone, to try to clear some of the cobwebs from my brain and heart, but I also don't want to alienate her. I suppose Molly is about to be clued into the real Smith sooner than I wanted to let him out.

"Okay," she accepts without hesitation.

It takes Molly all of five minutes to be ready, and that is refreshing because all of the other women I've dated take up to an hour, even for a hike, which is where I tell her we're going. She joins me on the driveway, her own backpack slung over her shoulder, and I swing a leg over my bike.

"We're, uh ... taking your motorcycle?" She audibly gulps.

Her fear, tinged with the lust I see in her eyes, breaks my

tension and makes me chuckle. "Don't worry, I won't go too far over the speed limit."

Watching her pull my extra helmet onto her pretty blond ponytail and then swing a leg over behind me might be one of the hottest things I've ever seen. And when she wraps her arms tightly around my waist, the dumbbell of anger that was sitting on my chest seems to ease up.

Molly lets out a squeal as we take off, but I feel her relax into my body as I drive, winding the bike through the busier roads and then out toward the ocean. The state park is one I've visited often, and the closer we get, the more my grief seems to recede to just a painful twitch in my chest.

I'm thankful that Molly seems to intuit that I don't want to talk about it, that I just want her to be next to me, because when we arrive at the hiking path, she just follows my lead. We strap our backpacks on and begin to walk, into the tree-lined bluffs first and then up and up until the sound of the ocean becomes clearer. I know the point I'm trying to reach, and it takes some effort, but Molly never complains.

We work together, pointing out footholds, or I help hoist her onto the next level of terrain.

Finally, we're at the destination, and I help her up the small, jagged ridge of the Hoodoos, until we're standing atop the cliffs looking out over the ocean.

"This is beautiful." Molly exhales, gazing out onto the massive body of water with such wonder.

"It was one of my sister's favorite places," I tell her, looking out upon the waves myself.

The gaze of her hypnotic hazel eyes lands on my cheek, but I can't look at her. "You used to come here with Stephanie?"

We've never spoken about my sister, and yet I find it oddly comforting that Molly doesn't pretend she doesn't know her name. It would have annoyed me to have to explain the backstory, to introduce my twin posthumously, and I'm glad Molly doesn't make me do it.

I nod. "We summered out here in house shares for a few years together. Steph loved it, the idea of getting away from the city. She was in public relations, and was always on the go, but out here, she got to be still. This park was her favorite, climbing up here to these bluffs. She'd sit here for hours by herself, meditating or listening to podcasts. It's where I come when I need to feel her on the really bad days."

I've never admitted this much to anyone about Stephanie, not even my family. But Molly's calm demeanor and unassuming listening skills, they just soothe me. It's not easy to open up about my twin sister, but this is the easiest I've found it, in Molly's presence.

"Is this a really bad day?"

I gulp against the tears in my throat. "Yeah."

"Tell me about her," Molly suggests.

It's nice that she didn't ask me to tell her how she died, or ask about my sadness or grief. After losing someone so close to me, I notice the way people phrase things when it comes to grief. So many people want to focus on the sadness of things, how the person died or how it's devastated your family. Not a lot of people wanted to go back, to know about the goodness of my sister before this tragedy happened.

"Steph was ... the brightest light. She was spunky and so smart, she'd help a wounded animal one second and then be harassing a guy in gym class for making some rude comment about a girl's ass. My sister was the best of this world, a fighter with a heart of gold. She never gave up on people, no matter how many times they let her down, and she was the funniest person I knew. God, she could make a full-fledged comic piss his pants; I saw it one time. We had this connection, she and I, because we were twins. They say that whole 'I know what you're thinking thing' is a myth, but it's not. It's like having a piece of you walk outside your body, that's how in sync we were. And since she's been gone, it feels like I'm missing a piece of me."

I look out over the water, almost as if I might find that piece of me. It's not an exaggeration to say that it feels like a chunk of who I always thought I was ceased to exist the day Stephanie died.

"I'm so sorry you lost her."

Molly just comes up and hugs me, and even though I'm larger than her, even though my arms wrap all the way around her body, it feels like she's the one holding me. She's comforting me, there is nothing sexual or suggestive about this embrace. It's one person trying to soothe another's pain, and I break a little.

I bury my head in her shoulder and the black chasm of mourning that's overtaken my soul the past six months gives way. Sobs wrack me; silent, angry, devastating convulsions that leave me exhausted with each expulsion of energy.

After a minute or two, they stop, but I still hang onto her. It's the first time I've ever opened up about this, and it's strange that it's not to one of my family members, or someone like Peter.

But in a way, I kind of knew it would be Molly. Stephanie knew how I felt about her. I can almost feel her grinning down on me, in a told-you-so kind of manner.

It almost feels like my sister's last prank, the last act of stubbornness. She's putting us together, will force me to confess my feelings, and she's going to use her story to do so.

21

MOLLY

"Mol, we're playing tennis, let's go!"

Peter walks by my chair, hitting the top of it, and I'm roused from the dream-like state I was in. I've been baking in the sun for almost an hour, content to do absolutely nothing.

"Play with someone else, I'm relaxing." I pout, my body protesting any form of physical activity today.

"No. I need a partner," a voice whispers in my ear, sending tingles racing all over my body.

Well, now I'm most certainly not lethargic whatsoever. Smith stands to his full height, his eyes hidden behind dark sunglasses, and he looks like he could be on the courts at Wimbledon with that sharp all-white tennis outfit. He looks absolutely edible, all Hamptons glamour, as his gaze stalks over me. Although I can't see those beautiful blue eyes, I can feel them on all of my most sensitive parts.

It's been three days since our date, and three nights of making out in the bathroom at night. We flirt in hidden corners and hallways throughout the day, he'll leave me little notes under my pillow, and we brush our teeth together every night.

After that, well, let's just say those make-out sessions haven't stayed PG. There have been hands under shirts, some flirting with the waistline of pants, and a shirtless Smith. Certainly a sight to behold.

He says he wants to take me out when we're in the city this week, as we'll have more freedom to actually go on a date. I kind of like the sneaking around, as much as it gives me paranoia. I know it would be weird to these people, who I all met through my ex-boyfriend, if I started dating another one of their friends. The thought of them finding that out has unease sloshing through my stomach, so I'm completely fine just keeping this to ourselves for now.

"I have to go change, then." I blink up at him.

"You could play in that." Those devilish, dark orbs rake down my body.

I might be wearing a bathing suit, but Smith might as well be untying it with his eyes, that's how naked I feel. It's sinful, how much lust this man can pack into one sentence.

I roll my eyes. "I'll be a few minutes. But I don't want to hear anything about being paired with a lame partner, you got it?"

"I would never." He smirks and makes his way off to the court.

How different our conversations are from just a few weeks ago. Smith was making comments not too long ago about how I couldn't afford the loser's prize of a lobster dinner, and now we were shoving our tongues down each other's throats in the bathroom every night. Life is indeed strange.

I hop off my beach chair and head inside to put on a pair of workout shorts and a tank top. I definitely don't have anything professional to play in, not like Smith, but I could make do. That thought keeps hitting my mind, how much things have already changed between us. I still can't believe he shared so much about his sister on that hike at Shadmoor.

It was clear, from the moment I encountered Smith that morning, that something was wrong. At first, I thought it was me. I thought I'd done something wrong, said something wrong on our date, and that he was just avoiding ever having to interact with me again. That had sunk my heart fast, little chunks splintering off and plunking into my soul.

But I was thankful he'd let me tag along. It was a small gesture that this wasn't about me or our date, and I honestly wasn't going to press. I was just going to hike with him. Except once he started opening up, I was even more shocked. I was around the group when his twin sister, Stephanie, had died tragically. It was awful. I went to the funeral with Justin, even though I felt weird being there because I thought Smith hated me. I remember how Smith cried over the casket; I'm sure that was the most pain I've ever seen another human in.

Clearly, and for obvious reasons, Smith is still completely broken up about her death. It doesn't seem like he's coped at all, and I was honored he put his trust in me. I have a feeling he doesn't talk about her much, though I didn't ask or push. I let him tell me what he wanted to get off his chest. In a very short amount of time, I think it bonded us closer to each other.

I walk back out of the house in my tennis match gear, holding a spare racket that someone had put on the kitchen table.

"We ready to do this?" Marta flexes her muscles like she's in for some healthy competition.

My sneakers hit the green, bouncy material of the court floor, and I nod to her. "Yeah, I'm ready to have some fun."

"Fun? We're getting lobsters out of this. We're about to clobber you guys." Peter puts his best mean face on, but it doesn't really work.

Peter is a doctor, with manicured hands and a kind of metrosexual-style to him. He's anything but intimidating.

"We're going to whoop their asses." Smith winks at me, and my heart skips a beat.

A man like that should not be allowed to wink at an innocently unassuming woman.

The match starts out slow, with Marta serving, and the first three tries ending in faults. When we finally do get going, the sun beating down on the court; it becomes a fun jest of words and thwacking. Peter keeps making these very girly moans each time he hits the ball, and everyone, including the spectators sitting on the side of the court, keep laughing our heads off.

Smith and I are a good pair, with him taking the back of the court and me up front. His legs are longer to catch the stray shots before they go out, and I have pretty good reflexes to react to the bloopers Marta keeps trying to trick me with.

"Good point, partner," he says after I whack the ball to a place Marta can't reach, and it bounces twice on the court.

Smith walks past me, brushing a hand over my hip. My skin turns to goose bumps in under a second, even though it's about eighty-five on this court. He's taunting me, flirting with me right here in the open, and knowing I can't do anything but blush.

Well, that and be totally flustered. Because two serves later, he swats my ass with his racket, congratulating me.

"You're killing it." He winks, and my panties are soaked.

That might as well have been his hand caressing my butt cheek, that's how much friction he sends burning over my ass and between my thighs.

"Stop." I cut my eyes at him, not able to keep the embarrassed grin off my face.

No one outside the vicinity of our hushed voices is any wiser to what's going on, but if he keeps this up, I won't be able to control my own actions.

"It's not my fault your perky ass is on full display, bent over every time a serve is coming toward you," Smith whispers.

It probably looks like we're having a quick team pow-wow to discuss strategy, when in reality, the man is initiating me in foreplay in plain view of five other people. This flirty, *friendly* version of Smith is way more dangerous than the guy who used to hate me. Or pretend to, according to him.

We continue our game, and it's our serve on forty-love for the winning point. Smith lines up the shot, and my God is he a dazzling sight. I have to shield my eyes from the sun, which is gleaming down on his tan body, as he stretches to his full height to whack the ball. His shirt pulls up, revealing the line of abs I've recently been feeling up in our shared bathroom.

The point is hard, with a dozen or so back and forths over the net. At one point, I think Marta's got me, because she sends a short little hit over the net and I have to sprint to catch it. On a wing and a prayer, I heft all my might into my arm, batting the ball with my racket. It just barely goes over the net, and Marta dives for it.

But she's too late, and it bounces again, then out of bounds.

"Yes!" I pump my fist, jumping up and down.

Though I may be an agreeable, and some may even call me meek, person, I love winning a hard fought competition.

"Damn it!" Peter stomps on the other side of the court.

"*Yeah!*" Smith runs up beside me.

I offer my hand up in a high five, which he completely bypasses to instead scoop me up into a victory hug. He twirls me around, and then slowly lowers me down his body. Every one of my curves hits every lean muscle on the front of his body, and by the time my sneakers touch the court, my nipples are so hard, they could cut glass.

"You fuckers owe us lobster." Smith lets go of me, clapping in Peter's direction.

But I'm barely aware of the congratulations being wished upon us by everyone else. No, I can only focus on the pounding between my legs, the blood that has rushed to one ball of nerves right between my thighs.

Smith and I have kept things pretty PG up until now, but he was coming on stronger with the full effects of his charm.

There was no way I'll be able to withstand it for much longer.

22

SMITH

My hand is just not cutting it anymore.

I lie in my bed, staring at the ceiling, knowing that Molly is right next door. We just got back to the beach house today, after we both spent a couple of days in the city. One of those nights was spent walking through Central Park together, and we called it a date, but it ended with me putting her in a cab.

I want to be respectful, to not rush us, and it felt like a lot of pressure since we were alone. I knew that if I asked her to come back to my apartment, things would not have stopped at kissing. They wouldn't have even stopped at foreplay. And I wouldn't have let her leave my bed, because I've fantasized about it for so long. I want to do this right, to court her and show Molly how much this means.

But lying in the dark, just feet from her ... it was messing with my brain. And my balls.

When I hear the creak of a door in the hall, I jump out of bed, desperate at the chance to see her once more.

We had a cozy house dinner tonight in leiu of going out, but it meant that I had to keep my distance and not draw too much attention to our interactions. The entire time, I'd wanted to sit on the same couch as her, or flirt with her in the hot tub when all the girls put their bikinis on and hopped in post-sundae bar.

As I slowly pull open my door, I'm in luck, because a flash of blond is what meets me as I exit my room.

"Hey," I whisper, catching Molly's attention as she heads for the bathroom.

"Hi." She smirks, knowing where this is heading already. "Should I meet you in there?"

Sidling up to her, I put on my best seduction voice. "Or you could come in there with me."

I motion with a slight nod back toward my room, and Molly's eyes look past me, to my bedroom door.

"What happens if I go in there?" Molly asks, her quiet honesty always somewhat a shock to me.

I was used to women playing coy or playing games. There weren't many left like her who would just say what was on their mind.

Deeply, so she understands I mean this, I look into her hazel eyes. "If we go in there, I won't be able to stop at just a kiss, Molly. I've waited a long time for this, for you. I'm not trying to pressure you, but I'm not going to make promises I can't keep. If we go in there, I want all of you. I want you under me, moaning my name. I want to feel it when you come with me deep inside you, and I want you to look me in the eyes when you unravel. I've thrown you for a lot of loops, I know that. But I'm asking you to trust me once more. And know that I would never ... I will never hurt you. Not in there, and not in here."

I press my palm to her chest, feeling her heart hammer against my skin. This is my plea, the closest I can come at this point to revealing how I truly feel. It's only been mere weeks, but I feel more connected to Molly than maybe I've ever felt to anyone. It's so strange to think that I've been waiting over a year to confess to her, and here I am, doing it. Not just because I desperately want to take her back to my bed, but because I desperately want her to feel this way, too.

Her eyes have melted to liquid pleasure, and I think she's half-drunk on my words alone.

"Is this too fast?" Molly says this maybe more to herself than she does to me.

I shrug. "Maybe. Maybe for both of us. But, and this sounds cliché coming from me, life is too short. I want this, Molly. I want you."

She waivers for another second and then seems to make up her mind, offering me her hand. I take it, her grip so dainty in my big hand, and lead her to my bedroom.

The instant the door clicks closed behind me, I move toward her. My hands sweep into her hair, pure silk between my fingers, and I cover her mouth with mine. The kiss is all-consuming, passionate, but not harsh. It's languid and filled with anticipation, a clawing sense ripping at my chest. My heart is beating too fast, my lungs spasming with the thought that I'm finally about to have this woman in the way I've wanted her for such a long time.

Molly matches my tongue with each lap, my hands with each exploration of new skin. We've barely been alone with each other, haven't gone far past kissing, but tonight, there is no holding back. We're adults, we don't need months of working our way toward sex. I would never be able to stop myself anyway, Lord knows I've tried. It's all or nothing with Molly; I had to actively work on hating her so I didn't profess my love when she could never feel the same way. Now she can feel that way, and I can't pretend anymore. I want everything with her.

The moonlight is the only source of illumination for us, but I don't need it. I'll savor her body with my gaze another time, this first one is all instinct. Her pajama top comes off, a whoosh in the silent room as it falls to the floor. My cock jumps in excitement when I find she's not wearing a bra beneath, and my hands mold to her small, perfect breasts.

"*Oh ...*" Molly breathes, her head dropping back as I roll her nipples between my thumb and index fingers.

Her hands find my bare skin. The only pajamas I'd been wearing were a pair of thin cotton lounge pants. Her nails run down the rivulets of my abs, tickling me but also causing my balls to heave in anticipatory pleasure. I'm so turned on, but more than that, my mind and heart are involved, too. This isn't just fucking that's going to happen here, it's ... well, I can't explain it in terms that are understandable. It gives me that feeling of enormity, of being very big in my own small world.

With her hands dancing dangerously close to the waistline of my pants, I move us to the bed, lightly pushing her so that she falls back.

"You have no idea how many nights I've dreamed about you, right here," I tell her, before picking up one of her legs and planting kisses on the inside of her calf.

"Me too." She sighs, wriggling as my teeth nip at the sensitive skin behind her knee.

"I want to taste every part of you," I say between kisses, alternating between her legs.

Her skin is hot and smooth and smells faintly of peaches.

"Smith," She moans after a while, and Jesus Christ, does it sound like heaven when she groans my name like that.

I know she's impatient, that I could stay here all day and simply savor each inch of her. Reaching for her shorts, I pull them slowly down, searching to find her eyes in the dark. When I do, they're locked on mine, our breathing suspended between us. Her underwear comes with them, and then she's naked, completely bare for me.

The ravenous beast inside struggles to gain footing over the slow, controlled portion of me. On one hand, I want this to last. I want to show Molly gentle compassion and cherish her the way she deserves. On the other hand, I can smell how wet she is for me, and my cock is tingling to pound relentlessly inside her.

"Please. I need you." She pulls at my wrist, and I come down on her, her bare pussy connecting with the material of my pants as she locks her legs around me.

"You're so fucking beautiful." I growl, the leash slipping off my control.

Grinding my hips into her, the friction nearly causes my eyes to roll back in my head. I want to push my pants past my hips and slide right into her, but I know I want to do something first.

"I need to taste you."

Moving the short distance down Molly's body, I don't hesitate before licking right up her center. Her hips shoot up off the bed, and I lock them down, planting my hands strongly on either side of her waist. My mouth devours her, and the moans turn to yelps above me. We should probably be quiet, considering there are five people in this house who have no idea that we're even speaking to each other, much less elbows deep in each other's naked bodies, but I don't even care at this point.

"Please, get inside me. I need to feel you inside me." Her words are quiet but fierce, and in seconds I'm whipping off my pants and boxers.

All to pause, gripping my cock at the base just millimeters away from her dripping, swollen pussy.

"Shit." I don't remember where I put my condoms, if I even have any.

Aside from Molly, who I thought I had no shot with coming into this summer, sex has been the furthest thing from my mind. I haven't been having any, and I guess I'm out of practice in the preparation because *I'm the guy*. I should have the protection.

"I'm sorry, I don't ... fuck, I feel like a dick. I don't have any condoms."

I drop my head to her shoulder and roll off of her, feeling like a teenager just seconds away from glory, all to spoil it.

The gentleman in me corrects course in less than a second, climbing back on top of her to make her come. "Let me make you feel good."

I wanted to feel her do that around me, but I'd never leave her high and dry. The sounds and taste of her will be enough for now, because I'm such an idiot.

But Molly doesn't let me venture back down.

"It's okay, I'm on the pill, and I'm clean. Please. I want you, Smith."

"Are you sure? I haven't been with anyone for a while, but I'm clean too."

Each word hits me in the chest like a sledgehammer, because that's a lot of trust to put into a person. I know how intimate it is to have sex with someone without protection, and I don't need to have talked to Molly about this to know how sacred that is to her. The fact that she wants to do that with me?

Leaning down, I brush a gentle, calming kiss to her lips, and her arms wind around my neck. With our noses pressed together, I slide into her.

And the feeling is more soul-bending, more intense than I could have ever imagined. We're breathing the same breaths, moving as one body, beating within the same heartbeat. I've had women, more than enough, in my life, but this is something entirely different. It feels like an out-of-body experience, like the pleasure is a secondary sense and my first is to just experience Molly in every way.

Normally, I like to talk during sex. My mouth and teeth like to move, I like to feel her curves. But right now, all I can seem to do is pump my cock in and out of her, and lock my gaze on her eyes. Our arms are wrapped around each other, so much so that when I feel her orgasm begin, I feel her shake from the tips of her shoulders down to the ankles that are wrapped around my back.

Molly comes wordlessly, her body shivering with pleasure, her head tipped back into the pillow. She looks like a work of art, something that should be housed in the most famous of museums. Every time I think of delight, of bliss, this is the moment I'll recall from this point on.

"I always knew ... I always knew ..." I seem to gasp on the words as my balls contract, cum bursting from my tip.

My climax steals through every cell, every nerve ending, a surprise as I'm still watching Molly unravel. I go still, spilling myself into her. The fact that I'm bare makes it last a lifetime, her pussy pulsing with each twitch of my cock.

When I'm finally able to suck in a lungful, when the white dots clear from my vision, I feel Molly's lips pressing against my jaw, my cheeks, my nose. We're still wrapped in each other, and I take her lips, tasting salt. Was she crying?

I'm about to ask, but she thrusts her tongue in my mouth, and I don't even have the chance to soften. Rolling over, I take her with me until she's straddling my lap.

"Remember those dreams I told you about? One of the biggest ones is having you ride me."

23

MOLLY

I snuck out of Smith's room at five a.m., much to his protest.

He'd backed me against the door, all but blocking my exit, and kissed me until I was half convinced to just let him lure me back to bed.

But we'd agreed that this is definitely not the way the rest of the house should find out about us, and I really needed to get my head on straight before I could tell other people, especially Heather, that I was seeing Smith.

I'd tiptoed back to my room and passed out until eight thirty, when my body woke me up because I'm no longer a college student and can't sleep until noon every day.

Surprisingly, I was the first one down in the kitchen, so I started breakfast for everyone. I found a box of Bisquick in the pantry, along with some chocolate chips, and poured it all in a mixing bowl. The task is menial; it helps me focus on something other than the blush that keeps creeping up my neck every time I think of Smith between my legs.

My God, I could fantasize about that man all day. Now I know how lethal he is, and I don't think I'll ever be able to concentrate on anything ever again. It was hard to think straight when I simply thought he was hot and wondered what kissing him would be like. Now that I know that sex is that freaking spectacular with him? I'll be a one track mind for the rest of eternity.

And it wasn't just that he was extremely skilled in the sack. The way he looked at me, held my eyes when he'd been inside me, whispered sweet nothings in my ear ... last night did not feel like a rebound or a one-night stand. My body isn't the only thing melting to Smith's charm. No, my heart is venturing into dangerous territory.

"Morning!" Marta chirps as she comes in, clad in the smallest silk nightgown I've ever seen.

Not that it looks slutty at all, no, in fact she looks tasteful and elegant. I'd just look foolish in something like that.

"Good morning. I'll be done with these in a second. Mind popping some sausage in a skillet?" I ask her.

"Funny, I just had my morning sausage." She wiggles her eyebrows at me, and I nearly choke on my tongue.

There is no way anyone knows, but I'll still be sweating all morning, and probably the rest of the week.

Ray rolls his eyes as he lumbers in behind her, chuckling at his girlfriend's antics.

"Smells good in here." Heather kisses my cheek as she passes the stove and goes for the coffee.

Jacinda comes in next, walking to the fridge to grab the juices and start setting the table, and she's followed by Smith.

The temperature goes up ten degrees just from him being in the room, and I fidget uncontrollably as his deep voice greets everyone good morning.

"Looks like someone ended his dry spell for the summer. I'm surprised it took you this long to bring a chick back." Peter laughs as he walks into the kitchen, clapping Smith on the back.

I have to bite the inside of my cheek to keep from reacting.

Not only does it make me want to giggle, Peter thinking that Smith brought some random back here, but him mentioning Smith's bedroom activities from the night before has my core tightening. I should be too exhausted to be embarrassed. The man kept me up until five a.m. and made me come *multiple* times, but just remembering his skin on mine has me wetter than I've ever been.

"Yeah, well, a man has his needs," Smith boasts, and I'm not sure I like the tone in which he says it.

I know he's probably trying to throw everyone off our scent, but this sounds like a conversation the two of them have had before.

"And from the sounds of her, she was one wild chick." Jacinda snorts. "I swear, you must have been doing something right."

I'm so flustered, I flip a pancake clear into the burner, missing the pan completely. "Oh, shit!"

"No worries, I'll scrape the batter out later." Marta smiles at me, none the wiser.

No one is aware that I'm the, apparently, *very loud* woman Smith had sex with last night.

"He's back, baby. This guy was a dirty stay-out or had someone new in his bed every other weekend last summer. Where is she, huh?" Peter peers around, and suddenly I'm overcome with a nauseous feeling.

I knew Smith had many ladies in and out of his life, I'd experienced it firsthand when Justin and I started dating, but I didn't necessarily want to hear that he'd slept with half the Hamptons last summer.

"Put her in a cab this morning. I didn't need a clinger." Smith sounds so nonchalant, and shame pricks at my tear ducts.

Is that his usual procedure? Will I be just like one of those girls, sneaking out of his room? I suddenly feel like a moron, because I let him lure me into his room and put up no objections when things moved fast. I was a big girl; I knew what my body wanted and while I didn't regret having sex, it now felt like I was just one of the many notches in his bedpost.

"Atta boy. Ah, to be young and virile again." Peter puffs out his chest.

"You're the same age as him." Jacinda rolls her eyes. "And shouldn't you be boasting about the elegant, strong female who occupies your bed every night?"

Peter moves toward her, catching her up in a hug. "Of course I am, sweetheart. I'm so grateful that you're the ball and chain to my old man ways."

Marta snickers. "Well, personally, I think it's kind of whorish of you, Smith."

Smith doubles back as if she's wounded him. "Ouch, Mart. Relax. Both parties had a wonderful time."

And now he was all but spilling secrets about our bedroom session last night. I feel like I'm going to be sick, so I scoop the last of the pancakes out of the skillet and turn off the flame. Hastily making myself a plate, I don't even give a verbal excuse as to why I'm fleeing the kitchen with my breakfast.

I eat in silence by myself out on the front porch, my heart breaking with every passing second. Smith is the first man I've been with since Justin. Since the man I kind of thought I'd marry left me high and dry. That was an emotional thing for me, even if it was a weekend night conquest to Smith Redfield.

But more than that, I thought what had happened between us really *meant* something. To hear him speak about what happened in the privacy of his bedroom last night like that, it crushed me.

Possibly even more than my breakup with Justin. Which not only made me feel sick, but terrified me more than I could even admit.

24

MOLLY

Midweek, Smith and I travel back to the city together.

Oh, don't get me wrong, he doesn't drive me straight from the Hamptons house to my apartment. No, I have to take a cab to the Jitney station, where he then picks me up so none of the roommates see that we drove back together. Not that anyone would question that. They'd think Smith was finally doing something nice out of the blue for me, but I don't think any of them would say to themselves, "yeah, Smith and Molly are totally jumping each other's bones."

I suppose I'm just getting tired of the sneaking around. For the last week, we've been tiptoeing around the house after hours, texting each other while we all sit in the same room, and having to pretend like we still mildly loathe one and other.

After sulking in my breakfast for an hour outside by myself that morning Smith and Peter had the one-night-stand conversation, I gathered my confidence back up and headed to my room to change. While up there, Smith knocked on my door and let himself in. He'd kissed me with the intensity I'd imagine exists on the surface of the sun, and I was a goner. I feel weak for not addressing things, yes, but ...

It all just feels too good. And for someone who had her life turned upside down and shattered just months ago, I deserve to feel good for a little while. Even if I'm deluding myself.

It's getting harder and harder not to tell Heather. She's my best friend and has watched me go through probably my most brutal breakup ever this year. Night after night, she encourages me to dance with random guys at bars, or take one of them home. And I know she thinks I'm not doing it because I'm still pining for Justin, which I kind of was. Up until two weeks ago. But now? The reason is because I'm totally falling for Smith Redfield and that sounds absolutely insane to say.

Isn't there that saying? It takes you half the time of the relationship to truly get over someone. With that logic, I still have another three or four months to mourn Justin and I before moving on. Everything before that would be considered a rebound, right?

Except, nothing with Smith feels like a rebound. When we're together, it feels like so much *more*. That realization both scares and excites me. He's not the man I thought he was, well, not entirely. I always knew he was hardworking and dedicated, that he'd come from a big family and humble roots. But I didn't know how sensitive he was, how hard it is for him to open up. Before, when he was a sullen, taunting menace, I thought that Smith Redfield was an egotistical prick who treated women like his disposable sex objects. Now, I knew the truth.

When we were up on the cliffs, he told me he hadn't slept with anyone in months, hadn't dated since before Stephanie died. His playboy image was just that, an image to keep others at arm's length.

I also saw how caring he was with his friends. He changed the oil in Marta's car last weekend and went out of his way to pick up Jacinda's favorite meal from in town when she wasn't feeling good. Peter had let it slip that he'd stayed in the city an extra day last week to help out one of his nephews in a basketball tournament.

Sometimes, I wonder how I never saw this? Was I just so enamored with Justin that I couldn't recognize the defense tactics Smith was putting up? No. He was pretty damn convincing that he loathed me. But the minute he told me how he felt, it was like a switch flipped inside me. My heart tilted its gaze and thought, "oh, *there* he is." I don't know why I couldn't see it before, but with each passing day, conversation, and intimate moment, it's becoming clearer that there may truly be a lasting relationship between me and him. One that could surpass any I've ever had before, including the one I had with his best friend.

He invited me over to his apartment tonight, said he'd be cooking me a gourmet meal. Just in case, I brought a side of my garlic scalloped potatoes, a carrot cake with cream cheese frosting, and well, I also made my mother's famous corn casserole. I just couldn't help myself, a man had never cooked for me, and I also hated showing up places empty-handed. It's against my nature.

Smith's building is much fancier than mine, he even has a doorman. I checked in and he sent me up in the elevator. I find his door and knock, my heart imitating my fist.

"Hi." I smile, almost shyly, as he opens the door to his apartment to let me inside.

It's the first time I've been over to his place, or either of us has visited where the other lives permanently. Now that I've seen his building, I'm not sure I'll ever let him come to mine. Not that my impression of Smith hasn't changed; I used to think he was a pretentious snob, but now I see it's all been an act.

"Hi." He gathers me in his arms despite my hands being loaded down with bags, and kisses me like we'll do it forever.

I think that's what gets me most about this *thing* we're doing. It doesn't feel temporary. With every kiss, every touch, the more we fall into bed together, it feels like we're creating something to last a lifetime.

"Did you bring the entire food selection of Manhattan to my apartment? I told you I was cooking." He takes the bags out of my hand as I try to calm my erratically beating heart.

"I've seen you cook at the beach house, and the extent of your arsenal is cereal. I thought I'd just help out." I smile sheepishly.

Smith turns his head, my gaze following to his stainless steel and gray-cabineted state-of-the-art kitchen. "Well, that's probably a good thing because the only thing I've managed to do well is roast the chicken."

"Good, I brought everything else." I laugh. "I still appreciate you cooking for me. You did not have to do that."

"I wanted to challenge myself ... for you. You deserve to be treated well." I swear, Smith Redfield is standing in front of me, blushing.

A timer goes off on the stove, and Smith all but jumps. "Let me grab that. Make yourself at home! I'll pour you a glass of wine."

He's adorable sprinting off to the kitchen to tend to his chicken, which I feel like he probably worked all day on. A warm, tickling sensation steals over my cheeks and chest, because it's sweet the way he wants to impress me. Justin never did anything like this, it was all fancy gifts and wining and dining but never something that actually caused him physical effort. He used his credit card to impress me, which now that I look back on it, was only temporarily impressive. If I was honest, the schmoozing and new money act was getting old even before he took off on me.

Speaking of Justin, that's the first time he's crossed my brain in weeks. I've barely thought about my ex with all of this Smith stuff going on, and with the way he makes me feel, I've barely noticed the usual twinges of a broken heart. In fact, I'd say my heart is the least broken it's ever been. Smith has taken it, repaired it, and made it *his*.

I glance around his apartment, which has to be the size of my parent's ranch in Linden. The whole great room is open concept, which is unheard of in New York on my, or a lot of people's, salary. The front door opens into a large room with a flashy kitchen to the left, a living room with a massive black leather sectional to the right, and a hallway with more doors off to the side. And on the back wall, well not a wall, is a floor-to-ceiling window view of one of the harbors in Manhattan. The water below is inky black, but the lights from the boats and street illuminate it.

Smith's place is beautiful in a manly way, all clean lines and dark colors. His hardwood floors gleam and there aren't many personal effects, but it smells like his sandalwood cologne and there is a big framed picture of Frank Sinatra on stage to the right of his flat screen TV. Now that I listen, Frank is crooning softly in the background, and it makes everything feel more romantic.

"Your place is really nice," I tell him, moving into the kitchen.

"Thanks. I know it's not exactly homey ..." Smith trails off, handing me a glass of white wine. "But it does the job."

"I'd like the full tour, before or after dinner." I can't help but stare at him, he's just so freaking *hot*.

"Oh, I'll show you *all* the rooms." His eyes flash with something devilish.

I shouldn't be surprised by that each time I see him, but he really is drop-dead gorgeous. And tonight he's in jeans and a T-shirt, the most relaxed version of himself. His raven-black hair is messy, like he's been running his fingers through it, and there is at least two or three days' worth of stubble on his cheeks. Sometimes I have to pinch myself that this is the guy I'm sleeping with.

Not that we're doing much sleeping. We've been going at it like animals or horny teenagers; the minute the bedroom door closes, we're all over each other.

I sip on my wine, watching as Smith tries to get dinner wrangled. He's so cute, but I can't help that something has been nagging at me since we got home from the beach house.

We've not talked about the way Peter keeps teasing him about his conquests, but it's starting to weigh on me. The more Smith brushes it off with some playboy comment, the more I feel slighted. The more he acts like this is his MO, the more I start to wonder if what we have is truly genuine.

"That stuff you've been telling Peter," I start, because I don't want to mask my feelings anymore.

Smith turns around, oven mitts on his hands, and cringes. "I've been meaning to apologize for that. I should just tell him to shove it, that it's none of his business, but I thought that acting like it's just random hookups would protect us from any scrutiny. I thought that maybe he'd accept the answer more if I fed into, if I acted like—"

"Like a bro who was just banging random chicks?" I say, completely failing at keeping the hurt out of my tone.

Smith is in front of me in a second flat, those denim blue eyes searching mine. "I'm sorry. Shit, I should have seen this. I hurt you with that stupid crap, didn't I? I should have just kept my mouth shut, or told them? Is it time that we told them?"

I shrug, feeling vulnerable for bringing it up but also comforted that he realizes he did something wrong.

"I don't know. I like how things are right now, I just don't love that you need to cover it up that way with Peter."

"I won't do it again. Shit, I'm sorry, Molly. I just didn't want anyone to catch on and thought I'd sacrifice my own image to keep yours intact. I know you feel weird about people finding out …"

Smith keeps rambling on, but I'm caught up in my own thoughts. On one hand, I don't want to tell the others. It's less complicated how it is right now, and then we'd have to explain about Justin, and what if he somehow found out? Not that I should care what he thinks, and he has no say in who I date now, but it would still be strange.

And on the other hand, I kind of do want to go public. I want to be able to hold Smith's hand without sneaking off into a corner. How nice would it be to not get heart palpitations each time I sneak down the hall to this room?

"Okay. Okay, it's okay." I touch his arm, trying to soothe him. "Let's just eat dinner, yeah? We talked about it, and now I want to have a nice night."

He blows out a breath of relief. "Okay, yeah. That's all I want. I even cooked the chicken properly, or at least I think I did. It might collapse on itself when I cut into it, like Clark Griswold's turkey, but aside from that."

"It looks delicious. What can I help put on the table?" I try to move us past the awkwardness of the Peter conversation.

"Nothing, you sit. I'm supposed to be waiting on you, that's how tonight goes."

"And what? I'm supposed to wait on you if you ever come over?" I chuckle as I move to the dark, circular wood table with a view out the wall of windows.

"No, you're supposed to sit there looking gorgeous and then

let me get you naked after dinner. Don't you know how dating works?" Smith winks at me as he brings the first tinfoil-covered bowl over to the table.

"That's *your* version of dating." I smirk at him.

"And it's the only version of dating you're doing, so get with the program."

He bends to kiss me, slipping his tongue in and surprising me. A warm feeling spreads over my chest and abdomen, and I kind of want to skip right to the naked part.

Yes, this is the only version of dating I'm doing. What shocks me more is that I'm completely okay with being a one-man woman again, so quickly after ending a relationship.

But with Smith, it just feels *right*.

25

SMITH

All of the telltale signs are there.

Her shrugging me off last night and sleeping in her own bed alone. The way she'd blinked too many times when I chose to sit at the other end of the table at the restaurant all the housemates ate dinner at last night. How she'd side-eyed me across the dance floor at the bar we went out to after. I could practically feel Molly wishing I would acknowledge her.

It's been a couple weeks since we started our secret little tryst? Affair? Fling?

I know I was the one who suggested it, because I didn't know how to deal with violating bro code or becoming the cliché in the group. I didn't want to put Molly in the position of becoming that girl, the one who dated around a friend group. Because she was so far from it. But aside from Marta, no one knew my true feelings for her, or how long they'd been there. They would demonize me, say that I was some big bad wolf who'd shacked up with Justin's girlfriend the minute he departed from the US. They'd think Molly was weak for succumbing to my charm. It was always the narrative that was painted on me, and I wanted to live in our bubble while we could. Get to know each other without the outside judgment.

And if I was being completely honest with myself, I'm scared as fuck. I knew I was half in love with her *before* I got to feel her, kiss her, laugh with her into our pillows late into the night. Now? The enormity inside my chest felt impossible. How could I keep living with this big of an emotion lodged in my chest? I'd never been in love before, never told a woman those words. I didn't know how to have a relationship that wasn't built on surface-level attraction. If I went public with this, it would force me to examine the very real, forever feelings I have for Molly. I wanted to do that so badly, but I also know that I have no idea how to do that. What if I fuck it up? What if she ... what if she didn't want to be all in with me?

But now I could see how it's driving a wedge between us, keeping this a secret. No matter what the outcome is, whether we stand the test of outing our connection or it fell apart shortly after, I can't do this to her anymore. I can't do it to myself. Selfishly, I want everyone to know that I am the one she is with. That when the tenth guy came up to hit on her at the bar, I could feel free to put my arm around her waist. That I could be the one to sit next to her at dinner, that we could be free to go to bed together and not have to sneak around.

Plus, Molly has basically told me as much. I can see how much it hurt her when I looked into those pretty hazel eyes at my apartment. I've become just another douche in her eyes, with the way I've been talking about my sex life to Peter.

She's had to endure Peter making comments about the women passing through my room. We've had to avoid touching when we go out to bars, or even being overly flirtatious.

I'm done hiding us for even one more minute.

We're spending the afternoon at the beach, the whole house, just swimming and reading and relaxing.

After diving into the water straightaway, I look back at the beach camp we all set up. It's the same one we've occupied the beach behind our house with since the beginning of the summer. A big tent that looks like one of those ones a soccer mom sets up on the sidelines. Towels galore. Three coolers full of food and alcohol and soda.

Peter and Ray are on the sand, throwing around a football, and Heather and Marta are sitting right where the waves come in, sunning their bodies. Jacinda is on a phone call, walking up and down the beach, and Molly is in her usual chair, reading another new book. I swear, she goes through five novels a week, and it's damn impressive. I never thought I could be turned on by a girl's reading habits, but here we are.

Marching out of the water, I head straight for her. Peter motions to me and yells, as if he's going to throw the ball, but I wave him off. My sights are set on my target, and she's got her nose buried in a book.

Two of the girls are walking back to our "camp" of sorts, but I'm still undeterred. My shadow falls over Molly, and she looks up, a genuine smile her first reaction. Then she catches my expression, and her face morphs into pure confusion.

"Smith?" she says.

The water droplets from my hair and body flick off onto the brim of her sunhat, and over the stark white coverup she's got on.

She's about to push up from the chair, probably to ask me what's wrong and why I look like a crazed animal, when I practically haul her up. I press my mouth firmly against hers and kiss her, in front of every single person on that beach.

The kiss is tender, yet intense, a show of emotions and feelings that not only do I want to portray to Molly, but all of the housemates. I'm tired of hiding, and I want everyone to know that we're dating. Seeing each other. *Exclusive*.

Well, not that I've asked her that, yet, but for me, it's exclusive.

"What the fuck?"

Jacinda's voice comes from somewhere to the left of us, and she sounds stunned and genuinely confused.

Releasing Molly's mouth, and smiling at her like we're both in on this hilarious practical joke, I hug her to me, not caring that I'm soaking her.

"Wait, you two? What ... what is going on? I ... what!" Peter's jaw may be somewhere down on the sand.

My head swivels between our housemates, and Molly is giggling into the crook of my shoulder. "I can't believe you just did that."

"I knew it! I fucking told you!" Marta turns around to point a self-satisfied finger at Ray.

"You were right." He shrugs, as if he's been hearing theories from her for a while.

"What? What? *What*?" Heather keeps saying over and over again.

I look down at Molly, a triumphant smile on my face, but my heart a little weary. "I hope that was okay."

"I was afraid if you didn't do something soon, I was going to have to give you a stern talking to." She presses up on her toes to plant a kiss on my cheek.

"A stern talking to?" I chuckle, because this woman couldn't be more adorable. "Most women would slap me in the face."

"Maybe I should still do that. Should we try? It would shock them even more." She crooks an eyebrow at me.

"Excuse me, what the hell is going on?" Jacinda walks right up to us, waving her arms frantically.

"We're together." I shrug, as if this is all completely normal business.

"I thought you hated her," Peter deadpans.

Molly bursts out laughing. "I thought so too, until he kissed me."

"He never hated her, he—" Marta is about to spill all the skeletons in my closet.

"Ah, I ... we connected while sharing the house. And started dating. And we really like each other. Well, I can't speak for Molly, but I'm really enjoying her company."

"Likewise." She grips my hand as she steps back, making us a unit.

"This is so weird." Heather shakes her head, still in disbelief.

"Anyone have a problem with it? Actually, I don't care." I laugh.

Marta kicks up sand as she runs over, flinging her arms around both of us. "I'm so happy."

Me too, I think as the three of us group hug.

I know there will be a lot of questions, and maybe even some words from Peter about dating our best friend's ex, but I just don't care all that much.

If it means I get to be with Molly, out in the open now, I'll take whatever scrutiny comes my way.

26

MOLLY

"Let's make a toast!"

Marta holds up her plastic cup, liquid sloshing over the edge.

We all hold our cups up, though we have no idea what she's toasting to. I giggle and sway, because we're all too many drinks in. We decided to stay in at the beach house tonight, which led to one too many alcoholic beverages at dinner and then another too many after. We then went in the hot tub, which led to night swimming in the pool, and now we're all huddled around the kitchen island, drinking drinks we don't need to be drinking.

"To Molly and Smith, for fucking behind all of our backs and being super loud about it!" Marta raises her glass even higher.

Everyone busts out laughing, and some of them even take a drink to that, while I just blush like crazy and Smith flips her the bird.

"You're just jealous." Smith's eyes are hazy with liquor, and he looks adorable trying to defend his, or maybe my, honor.

"I kind of am." Marta chuckles, snuggling into Ray's side. "That new relationship kind of sex is always the best. Not that you're not totally hot, babe, but there is something about those early days that makes the other person seem very irresistible."

Smith's eyes roam over my body and face. "She's irresistible all right."

Peter wolf whistles. "I seriously can't believe you two are banging. I'm still shocked."

"We're not banging. We're dating. Get your facts straight." Smith sips from the neck of his beer bottle, and I swoon so hard at the labels he's using.

I guess I never realized how much of a romantic Smith is. Not only in his actions, but the way he says things. The first night we made love—and yes, I call it that because what happened in his bedroom was way more than sex—I was stunned speechless. Not only from how he professed his feelings in the hallway, but how cherished he made me feel in his arms.

And then yesterday, when he stormed the beach and literally stormed *my* beach for the whole house to see ... that made my heart fall into a blushing and stammering mess just thinking about it.

"Even weirder. Though, I can kind of see it. You'll make him a better man, Molly, that's for sure. Cheers to Molly!" Peter toasts his cup in my direction.

I haven't said much tonight, choosing to just observe and laugh through most of it. Smith scooped me up in the pool and carried me around on his back, like we were flirty teenagers in high school or something. I just reveled in the carefree attitude of the group, sipping on my drinks and letting the buzz invade my veins.

It was one of those perfect summer nights that you never wanted to end. Though, I would call time whenever Smith wanted to, because I'd very much like to crawl into bed and use the confidence the alcohol is giving me.

"Can we order pizza? I'm starving!" Heather complains, hopping up on the counter to sulk in her bikini.

"Perfect idea!" Ray seconds, grabbing the menu from the drawer. "What should we get?"

"Meat lovers!" Peter snickers, and we all roll our eyes.

"You're a fucking child." Smith punches him in the bicep. "What about a large pepperoni and then a large mushroom?"

Jacinda walks over to Ray, glancing down at the menu. "I'm good with pepperoni, but mushroom is gross. No. Can we add mozzarella sticks? I love those."

"Um, why would you order mozzarella sticks with pizza? It's basically just another form of pizza. Cheese, with red sauce." Heather cocks her head to the side, confused about why we'd order the appetizer.

"I'm only in if we can get white pizza," Marta throws her two cents into the ring.

Smith makes a gagging noise. "Ew no, get out of here with your disgusting taste. White pizza is not even pizza."

"It is, too!" Marta's eyebrows slant angrily together.

"Yeah, it's so good. All that garlic, and especially when you put ricotta on it." Heather licks her lips.

Jacinda is shaking her head across the kitchen. "Uh-uh, I vote that it's not pizza. It's basically glorified garlic bread."

"What? You people are insane. Let's take a vote. Who thinks white pizza is real pizza?" Marta's head swivels around, trying to count hands while very drunk.

She, Heather, and Ray all have their hands raised, though I think Ray may only have his raised because he's worried about his girlfriend chopping off his balls if he doesn't agree.

"And who votes that it's glorified garlic bread?" Smith shoots his hand in the air.

Jacinda and Peter follow, and everyone looks around. The room is tied, and my best friend points at me accusingly.

"Hey, you didn't vote, you little abstainer!" Heather shrieks.

I get booed with a chorus of *you must vote, cheater* and *break the tie*.

"Okay, okay!" I hold my hands up in surrender. "I think it's ..."

I pause, not just for dramatic effect, but to really consider it. I love a good piece of pizza and don't usually mind what's on it.

"White pizza is definitely pizza." I nod my head, as if I'm giving a final answer on *Who Wants to Be a Millionaire?*

A bunch of boos and cheers mix, the room thrown into victory and loss, while Heather jumps down and scoops me up into a hug.

"Take that, motherfuckers! We're ordering it!" She points at Jacinda, Peter, and Smith.

Smith steals me away, pulling me into his bare torso and damp bathing suit. "You should have sided with me. There would have been rewards."

I chuckle and melt at the same time, because he's almost licking my earlobe with his tongue. "I have a feeling I'll get rewards no matter what."

His hands slide down to my butt, squeezing one of the cheeks. "You're not wrong."

"Hey, hey, get a room you two!" Marta yells, pretending to be grossed out at our PDA.

Smith hauls me into the air, so that I have no choice but to wrap my legs around his waist. "Maybe we will."

"But I want pizza." Drunk me realizes that the whole white pizza debate left me very hungry.

"Fine, we'll wait for pizza, but then I get you for dessert." Smith nuzzles his mouth into my neck.

"Oh my God, you guys are such hornballs. I love it." Jacinda cackles. "You know what? I think you're perfect together."

Her words make my lips break out in a goofy, huge smile. It

feels like we've been covering things up for a while, afraid of what everyone else will think, and it's comforting to know that they're in support of this.

"I do, too," Smith whispers in my ear, for only me to hear.

And that? That makes my heart break into a goofy, huge smile.

27

MOLLY

My lip is in between my teeth when Smith smoothly swipes a thumb over my jaw, jostling me from my thoughts.

"What's going on up there?" he asks, sitting next to me in one of two Adirondack chairs on my balcony.

Part of the reason I'd picked this room was for the balcony, I knew I'd like to sit and read out here some nights or mornings. The other housemates had been all for it, since every room in the house aside from our two has its own bathroom, and they preferred that luxury over this one.

"Just thinking about my students." I smile at him, lacing our hands together.

"About what, lesson plans for the new year? When does school start, another month or so?" Smith asks, as if it was that simple.

"Yeah, another few weeks. And I've gotten some lesson planning done already. But no, I worry more about how they're doing, emotionally."

"What do you mean?" Smith's eyebrows furrow together.

I sigh, knowing this is heavy but also wanting to explain to Smith what I worry about.

"A lot of my students ... they have rough lives during the school year. Domestic abuse, volatile family situations, drugs, alcohol, homelessness, and that's all just before they arrive at school and have to learn on very limited budgets with the system working against them. But at least during the school year, they get subsidized meals and teachers who are looking after their wellbeing. If I see bruising, if I hear about abuse, I can report it. But during the summer, they have no one looking out for them. A lot of these kids come back to school the next year in such bad shape, only for us to try to mediate some of that, and then they go into the next summer to more detriment. I worry every day about each one of my kids from last year, and about the ones I'll receive in my classroom when September starts. It's hard not to stress about them all the time. They're just kids."

My voice breaks on the last sentence, betraying the emotion I've been holding back. My heart aches for these children, because they didn't ask to be born into a world so harsh and cruel. I want to give them everything I can during the school year and still keep in touch with some through the summer. I do my best to make sure they're in state-funded camps or nonprofit programs that can at least get them out of the house for a few hours from June to September, but there are always multiple who slip through the cracks.

Smith shakes his head, looking out onto the ocean. "Jesus, I'm sorry. I didn't realize. That's a heavy burden to carry on your shoulders, but I wouldn't expect any less from you. You're a giver, a nurturer, and I'm grateful those children have you worrying about them. It tears me up that their own parents don't do that sometimes, or can't. It's fucked up, this world. It shouldn't be like this. But those kids are lucky to have someone thinking about them as much as you do."

I shrug, blinking back tears. "I just hate that they may be hungry, or in pain. That's not how childhood should be. You're right, it's a fucked-up world."

I don't curse often, but this seems as good a time as any.

"You'll be back with them soon. And you make a difference in their lives." Smith squeezes my hand.

It doesn't really matter what he says, I'm just glad he's sitting here listening.

"Sometimes, I doubt if I do. If I hear one of them was arrested, or caught up in a gang bust, I just get sick to my stomach."

Smith reaches one of his big hands over to cup my face. "You're doing everything you can. Sometimes, it's not enough, but that's not on you. That's just on this shitty world. You're the most giving person I know. Way better than me. Sometimes I wonder if I even deserve to breathe the same air as you."

I give him a look like that's a ridiculous thing to say, and then we both look out over the ocean. For some reason, even though I was just worrying like heck over my kids, Justin pops into my head. Because if Smith, who I've found out is genuine and kind and grieving, thinks I'm too good for him then where does that put me with Justin?

"Is it weird that I was with your best friend?" I ask him, though it may be an awkward topic.

We don't talk about it much, obviously, since it's a weird subject between us. But now that we're pretty much public, at least to the people who matter, I think it has to be addressed. I haven't thought about Justin since, well, probably since the first night I was falling asleep in my room in the summer house. Truly thought about him, not just when I was confessing how strange our breakup was to Smith out on the porch downstairs. That night, I'd let my heart yearn one last time, and then it was truly over.

I have formed genuine friendships with these people all on my own, and now I am falling in love with my ex's best friend.

There is a tic in Smith's jaw, like he's clenching it too hard, when I look over at him.

"Sometimes. Sometimes I wonder how you were drawn to a guy like him, but then I feel like a prick. Because it's discounting your instincts, and it's also discounting my best friend. Justin may look like a prick now, and Lord knows he has his flaws, but he was always a good friend to me growing up. I feel guilty sometimes, us being together, but it's a fleeting feeling. What I have with you ... I can't speak for you, Molly, but it feels like so much more than I've ever had with someone else."

That raw answer is like a cupid's arrow to my heart. "It feels that way for me, too. I often wonder if I'd held out, would I have met you instead? But then I have to thank that relationship, I guess, because it brought me here."

We're both quiet a moment, just gazing at each other, and there are so many things I want to say but am too afraid to blurt out. It's only been a few weeks, but Smith is right, whatever is between us feels so much bigger than whatever I shared with Justin.

"Sometimes I get irrationally jealous. You're sleeping in my bed, but I know that you were once in his." Those blue eyes burn with envy.

"It was nothing like your bed," I mutter, unable to help myself.

"What's that?" Smith perks up.

"Nothing." I clamp my lips shut.

"No, what did you say?" He leans forward.

I sigh, embarrassment flaming my cheeks. "I shouldn't even tell you this. It's ... I shouldn't talk about this with you. It's not kind."

"Molly." Smith's voice is a warning growl.

"Justin was never exactly concerned with my needs." I shrug sheepishly.

Smith tilts his head, and I see it when the lightbulb in his brain goes on. "He never made you come."

It's not a question, but I still answer. "No. He didn't."

It's not something I'm proud to admit, because I feel like a little bit of that is on me, too. I never made it known, what I needed, what I liked.

"But, I also never said anything. I went along with our sex life as if nothing was wrong."

Smith's eyebrows are angry slashes. "That is not your fault. Every man should make sure, guarantee, that the woman he's sleeping with has an orgasm. Every. Single. Time."

He sinks down onto the planks of the balcony right in front of me, like some kind of orgasm white knight. A white hot blush creeps from the crown of my head to the tips of my toes, thinking about the way he's made me come.

"Well, I have to remedy that for my girl. You will never be left unsatisfied."

"Your girl, huh?" I smirk against my suddenly dry lips.

I can't think straight when Smith is giving me those bedroom eyes, like a panther stalking his prey. *Me.* Those large hands begin to uncross my legs and sneak up the dress I have on.

"Smith, oh my God, not here." I try to close my knees, but his strong arms are spreading me open.

"Have I made you come every time we've been together?" His voice is raspy as he reaches up to my hips, his arms disappearing under my dress.

I gulp, unable to stop him now as he slides my panties down. I simply lift, giving him the access to pull them over my hip bones and butt.

"Yes." The tone that comes out is breathy.

"You better not be lying." He quirks an eyebrow as he brings my panties up to his nose and sniffs.

I swear, I'm staining my dress with my wetness. "I'm not."

"Good." Smith lifts my dress, and his head disappears under it.

It tents around the top of his raven-black waves, and my fingers white-knuckle grip the sides of the rocking chair in anticipation. I know that it's likely no one can see us from up here, and the sound of the ocean will drown out any noise, but it's still public. There is still that thrill that we're doing something a little naughty, and that only makes my pleasure build. It feels so wrong, and so right.

His hands wrap around my thighs from under me, holding me in place to the rocking chair. The minute I feel his hot breath against my wet slit, I'm bucking, a strangled moan swallowed in my throat.

Smith's tongue comes down on me, and I see white spots in my vision.

"The sounds you make drive me crazy." He growls, though I can't see him.

Not being able to watch, to see his next move, makes my orgasm build more quickly. His skilled tongue licks up my folds, swirling around and then nipping at my throbbing clit with his teeth. I wriggle against his strong grip, my breathing becoming more uneven.

"Smith," I whimper as he removes one of his hands and pushes two fingers inside me.

The pressure of his digits in me combined with the flat side of his tongue running up and down my clit has me clawing at the arms of the chair for release.

"Let go. I want to taste you come on my tongue." The dirtiness of his words kicks off my orgasm.

It moves through me swiftly, every limb and muscle

convulsing with the pleasure of it. Smith's head comes up from my dress, his blue gaze locked on my face. I'm moaning, I can hear it from some out-of-body experience, as I come around his fingers that are still lodged in me. My climax, tight and flowing all at the same time, wracks me, and Smith moves up so he can capture my mouth. When his tongue invades my mouth, it spurs my orgasm on evermore, and I arch my back into the erotic sensations.

After a few more moments, my body goes lax, spent and exhausted. Smith is still on his knees before me, watching my every movement. Then he says something that will stick with me forever.

"I could watch you come for the rest of my life. Any man who doesn't know the pleasure of watching that ... he's a fucking moron. You're incredible."

28

MOLLY

My toes are bright pink, my nails are a pretty teal, and I can't say I would have chosen either color.

But Heather called for some girl time, since she says she hasn't seen enough of me at the beach, and I've missed her, too. Now I'm lounging on her plush blush pink couch, my feet up on her mirrored and gold coffee table, with the *Sex and the City* movie playing in the background.

"I'll be a Samantha. Hot, single, and sleeping with every guy on both coasts when I'm well into my fifties." Heather nods sagely, as if she's already made up her mind.

"I could see it. Though you better not move to California, because then who will I eat pounds of Twizzlers with?" I chuckle, unwrapping a new one from the giant box her Mom still sends her every month from Costco.

"I would never. I can't leave my precious Manhattan. Or you, my Charlotte. And don't argue, you're totally a Charlotte. Although, maybe you're a Carrie, because you're definitely dating Mr. Big."

I roll my eyes. "Smith is not Mr. Big. He's nothing like Mr. Big."

Heather shrugs. "Eh, he's pretty smooth if you ask me. Has that business man persona, before he dated you he was evasive and the 'cool guy.'"

"You don't know him, he's really not like that," I say.

I'm on edge because we haven't talked about this yet, not in depth. Of course she's happy for me, after helping me through the fallout of Justin dumping me epically before he jumped on a plane, but I can tell my best friend has been apprehensive about my relationship with Smith. She's been letting me have my space and enjoy the summer, but I guess we're about to get into it.

"It just seems kind of quick." She quirks an eyebrow as she takes a sip of wine, not making direct eye contact with me.

"Do you have something you want to ask me, or are you just going to keep making judgy comments?" I sigh.

We've never been anything but honest with each other, and I know I've played my connection with Smith close to the vest. But I'm never one to beat around the bush, especially with Heather. She's like my sister; we've been best friends since I can remember, and sometimes I loathe her more than I love her. It never lasts for long, but apparently she's got a bone to pick with me, and I just wish she would do it.

Heather lets out a frustrated huff, then turns to me, tucking her legs up under her on the couch. "We started the summer hating the guy. I walked into the rental and he was already tormenting you. For the better part of a year, he made comments about your financial status, motives for dating his friends, and I even heard him mutter that one of your outfits was ugly under his breath. I just don't get how you can bury all of that. Maybe I'm missing something, but the guy seemed like a jerk for a really long time. You already got your heart broken by the ultimate narcissist, something I never saw coming, and I don't want to see you hurt again."

I know it's coming out of her concern for me, but I can't help that my defenses come up. "I know all of that, believe me I do. But you're going to roll your eyes at this. Smith confessed to me that it was because he secretly liked me, while I was dating Justin."

My best friend does just that, the whites of her eyes rolling all the way back into her head. "Puh-lease, give me a break. He used the old 'flirting on the playground' excuse to justify his behavior?"

"Yes, I know it sounds lame. But he claims he knew he had feelings for me since the first time Justin introduced us and wasn't going to intrude on his best friend's *territory*. That sounds like a bad way to put it, but you get what I'm saying. Anyway, he tried to distance himself from me, or make himself dislike me, but it was all an act. Don't worry, I took some time to analyze that as well. It's not like I just gave into the guy, Heather, you know me. But after a couple of weeks and really getting to talk to him, well, I don't know. This one is different. I think I might be in love with him."

I whisper the last part, and Heather's pupils go wide. "Wait, what!"

Now I need a gulp of wine. "He's just so much different than I ever thought. Smith is really romantic and genuine, and he's still lost in his grief. He's not the man you think he is, and I can't fully explain why because he's just different when we're alone. He's opened up in a way that no man ever has with me, and he's taken care of both my mind and my heart, unlike any other guy."

"And your body, I've definitely heard him taking care of that." Heather snorts, unable to help herself.

A scarlet blush creeps over my cheeks. "Yes, it's definitely the best I've ever been *taken care of*."

She slumps back. "I'm so jealous. Not just of the multiple

orgasms you must be having, but if he's as amazing as you say he is, then I want one."

"He is." I nod, my rose-colored glasses solidly in place.

"I just don't want you hurt. Justin did a number on you, and it's a little bit weird that you're dating his best friend. We used to trash talk the girls who did that."

"We did." I nod. "I kind of hate that I'm *that* girl, but I can't worry about it too much. I finally found a guy who I seriously think could be *the one*, and if that means I'm a cliché, then so be it."

"*The one*?" She all but gasps, grabbing her wineglass again.

"Yes." I meet her eyes.

"Wow, Mol, I'm a little shocked. But if you're happy, then I won't shank him for not doing his breakfast dishes a lot of days in a row. Though you should train him better."

That has me bursting out in laughter. "Oh my God, you're so right."

"I'm serious, though, Mol. I want you to be happy. But I just want you to be careful, too." She lays her hand over mine.

"I am. Don't worry, I'm not going into this blindfolded," I assure her.

The movie comes back from commercial, and we both turn our attention to the scene after the wedding, when Carrie has been jilted and is drinking vodka in Charlotte's house.

While I'm scared of becoming that, of being the woman who falls for a man who won't commit, I have to put it out of my head. Aside from the beginning of our relationship, Smith has done nothing to show me he won't sacrifice for me.

So I have to sacrifice my worry, my past trust issues, for him.

29

SMITH

"Dude, you have to make sure she can't see the candles from our room,"

Peter's voice is frantic, and his hands are shaking as he takes a lighter to probably the hundredth candle lining the sand.

"I told you, the girls are occupying her with some kind of chick happy hour. Marta knows the drill. You're in the clear until I tell her to come out here."

My eyes keep straying back to the house, to keep watch like I'm some kind of getaway driver. You'd think we were robbing a fucking bank, not setting up the scene for Peter to get down on bended knee and ask Jacinda to marry him.

He's been carrying around this diamond ring in his pocket for almost four months now, trying to think of the perfect time. When we secured the beach house, he knew this would be the perfect place, but then the question was, when? So, today is their four year dating anniversary, and he thought it would be perfect.

I think he could have asked her over a cup of coffee and she would have been ecstatic, but what do I know? Probably why I've never proposed to anyone.

"All right, I'm almost ready. How do I look?" He puffs out his chest, smoothing his hands down the white polo he has on.

"Like a fairy fucking princess." I smile like an asshole.

"Yeah, remind me not to make you my best man. Clearly, your pump-up speech sucks balls." He glares at me.

I clap a hand on his shoulder. "Brother, she's going to say yes. There is no doubt about that. Just take a deep breath and ask. You ready?"

He takes a few gulps, shakes out his limbs, and then squares his shoulders. "Yeah. Send her out."

I walk back up toward the summer house, my heart beating like a kick drum now, too. I don't know why I'm nervous, but it's a big moment for my friends. And kind of reminds me of how I'd like to do this, someday.

The girls are in the kitchen, blabbing about something, when I find Jacinda. "Jacinda, Peter needs you out back."

She's looking at something on Marta's phone. "All right, tell him to give me a few minutes."

"No, you need to go now." My voice takes on a strange tone.

All the girls' eyes look to me, questioning. Shit, I think I might have just spoiled the surprise.

"Okay, weirdo." Jacinda smiles at me like I might be speaking gibberish, but moves from around the counter.

She exits the French doors in the living room, and then Marta runs over to peek out the blinds.

"What's going on?" Heather asks.

"Peter is proposing," Marta screeches, and Molly and Heather fly to the window next to her.

All three of them are lined up, peeking out, and I go to join them. We watch as Jacinda walks toward the beach, and I see her body language the moment she catches on to what is happening. The girls gasp as Peter gets down on one knee, and I'm pretty sure Marta is sniffling away her tears.

"Oh my God, this is beautiful." Heather sobs.

Molly is silent, but I can feel her reach for my hand. I lace my fingers in hers, wondering if she's thinking about what I'm thinking about. Me, getting down on one knee. It's only been a matter of weeks, but I could see it. I can envision sliding a ring I buy especially for her onto her left hand.

Thirty minutes later, after we give them some space to cry and hug each other when Jacinda says yes, we're popping champagne bottles by the pool.

"To the happy couple," Ray toasts them, and we all drink from our flutes.

Heather and Marta swarm Jacinda, wanting to obsess over the two-carat diamond Peter just put on her hand.

Molly and I stand together, the sun setting behind her. It illuminates the white blond streaks in her hair, and I blink because she's just so beautiful. I could stare at her for hours, though many would find that weird. Including, probably, Molly.

"Do you want to get married?" Molly's eyes stray to Jacinda, who is admiring her new engagement ring.

I all but choke on the sip of champagne I just took. The liquid goes down the wrong pipe, and I frantically pound on my own chest as I cough like some kind of severe asthmatic.

"Oh my God, I didn't mean like that!" Molly's eyes swing to mine in full panic. "I meant like, does the idea intrigue you? I didn't mean ... me ... no, not ... you ..."

She trails off, and I can tell she's burning with embarrassment. Setting down my flute, I pull her into my arms, smirking as if I know it's my time to comfort the shame rolling its way through her stomach.

"I know you didn't mean it like that. It doesn't mean I haven't thought of it like that." I lower my face, almost touching the tip of my nose to hers.

"You have?" Those big hazel eyes blink in shock.

"I told you, Molly, I'm serious when it comes to you. Maybe not *that* serious yet," I nod in the direction of Jacinda and Peter, "but someday soon? Yeah. I'd like to get married."

I don't add that I want it to be to her, because it should be implied. I don't mean to freak her out, and the reason I choked is that it was like she was reading my mind.

Because I've thought about Molly walking down an aisle toward me, more times than I can count. I fell in love with her the first time I saw her, and so I've dreamed about a lot of things when it comes to her.

Molly's head, and hopefully her heart, are catching up to the things I never thought would become a reality. Now that they seem possible, I can't keep my mind from running away with all of the ways our lives could be joined together.

30

SMITH

Stefania is nearly done.

Campbell went home for the night, but I decided to stay in the dim light of only the bar lights on, working on some of the opening week preparations.

The hardwoods are in, gleaming and polished dark stained floors that cover the expanse of the restaurant. Tables, chunky wood with bright white table linens, cover the floors, while elegant gold-flecked chairs are pushed in underneath them. The massive bar that runs the length of the wall closest to the door was just finished two days ago, its intricate gold trimmings intertwined with the masculinity of the slab of natural wood we decided on for the top.

That's the best way I can describe Stefania; it's elegance mixed with strong, solid design. A dedication to my sister's personality.

From the pretty pendant lights over the bar to the sturdy fireplace on the other side of the restaurant, from the woodfire stove visible through the glass wall looking into the kitchen and the gold-framed photos of Italy hanging up around the space. It's a mixture of beauty and strength, and the whole thing came together exactly as I pictured it in my mind.

It was time to solidify the menu for our opening, now just weeks away. I couldn't believe we were here again, about to open up another restaurant and add another line to our résumés and headache to our days. There was always the pride that came with launching something new, but it meant more staff on my payroll, more critics knocking down or building up my name, and just a whole litany of problems Campbell and I would have to deal with.

Being in here, alone, before the world and the staff got to see it, was kind of my sanctuary. I came home from the Hamptons two days ago and have barely gone anywhere but here. We are in the finalizing stages, which means crunch time, and the timeline has been moving along smoothly. We have our liquor license, the chef's contract was signed, the public relations firm we use is pushing out invites to reviewers and society people alike.

And it means that I can think about Stephanie in a positive way, without mourning too much. Because if I let myself, this month would swallow me in grief.

Our birthday is coming up, and I don't know how I'll survive it. Aside from the days we were in college, and typically back on campus by that point, Steph and I had spent every one of our birthdays together. She would always buy me the exact present I never knew I needed, and I'd struggle for weeks to buy her something that I hoped would be meaningful.

This year would be dark, solemn, and the first reminder that I'd be growing older, while she would remain thirty for the rest of time. Steph will no longer move forward in life, and I'll be on my own in the truest sense of the word since we'd been born.

I try to focus on the words in front of me, *beef carpaccio and burrata salad and vine-ripened tomatoes with melon and prosciutto*, so I wouldn't have to keep thinking about the hardest pill I will ever have to swallow. We're importing some of the most authentic ingredients straight from Italy, much to Campbell's dismay.

But I wouldn't have it any other way. If we were doing this restaurant, we were doing it right.

And if I have to slave my days and nights away here in the city until this thing shined like the top of the Chrysler Building, then I'll do it.

There were only so many ways I could honor my sister, and this was the one I knew how to do best.

31

SMITH

I told my mother she could not throw me a birthday dinner; I wanted nothing of the sort.

But I would let her throw a Sunday family dinner, and I'd attend. So long as no one mentioned the word birthday, or party, or adding another year to my age.

And since I knew this night would be taxing even while my entire family was avoiding mentioning my birthday, I decided to invite Molly. She was quickly becoming the person who knew me best, who soothed me most, and whose simple touch could calm even my worst of moods.

Plus, it might draw my mom and her sisters off the scent of my sadness over my upcoming birthday without Stephanie. I'd rarely bring a woman home, and never one I was so serious about, so this would give them enough gossip to chew on for hours. Not that I didn't feel bad basically feeding Molly to the wolves.

"If you don't want to do this, we can just turn around," I tell her again, for probably the fifth time, as I drive my car down the familiar streets of Queens.

I feel her smirk as she turns to me and I keep my eyes on the road. "Is there some kind of wicked surprised waiting here for me that I should know about? You're so antsy."

My hand is on her thigh as I drive, the other on top of the wheel, and I run my thumb up and down her bare skin where her pretty white lace shorts stop.

"Just my aunts and sisters and cousins. They're like piranhas," I mutter.

She swats at my arm. "I'm sure they're lovely. And I'll be fine. I have to meet them sometime, Smith. I'm flattered you asked me to come to dinner."

I glance over at her while we come to a stop at a red light. "I want them to meet the woman who means so much to me."

And I shouldn't downplay that to her, or in my mind, just because I was anxious about my birthday coming up.

Molly's lips spread into a shy, small smile. "I can't imagine growing up with so many people in your house, let alone having siblings. It was always just me and my parents, and it was pretty quiet."

"Growing up in my house was like living in a zoo. Not only were there kids everywhere, but most of my parent's siblings live on the same block as us. It was a quiet day if there weren't ten or twenty relatives filtering in and out of the front door."

"Sounds fun," she says, sighing like she might have missed out on something in her own childhood.

"Well, you're about to find out," I say, pulling onto the street in front of my parent's house.

It's an old two-story on a tiny patch of land, just inches from the other houses on either side. The brown shingles and brown door have become weathered over the years, but that Italian flag still hangs proudly from the garage door, and my father's New York Mets insignia sign is stuck in the front garden among Mom's tulips.

My aunt Esther and aunt Francine are sitting on the front porch, smoking like chimneys, as we get out of the car.

"Smith! You're looking too skinny. Go in the kitchen, I brought sausage and peppers. Have a sandwich," Francine greets me like this.

Molly snickers in amusement under her breath, but she doesn't stay protected for long.

"Is this is the girlfriend? She's a blonde." Esther eyes her.

We have a lot of dark-haired, olive-skinned people in my family. Aside from Gianna, who is a bottle blond, my relatives aren't used to fair skin and light hair.

"Be nice," I warn both of them as I open the screen door for Molly and usher her inside.

As we move through the small rooms of my parent's house, we run into at least ten or fifteen more of my aunts, uncles, or cousins. They all either kiss our cheeks, ask who Molly is, want to talk business, or some other loud, obnoxious topic. I keep it moving, trying to get Molly to the one person who would be offended if we didn't say hi to her first.

Entering the kitchen, I see Burton leaning against the counter as my mom stands at the stove.

"Look who's here." My brother sticks out his fist to pound and I meet it.

"Came straight back," I emphasize, because I want Molly to make a good impression on my mom.

"She's much prettier than you mentioned, bro. Shame on you." Burton, my younger brother, kisses Molly on the cheek.

She chuckles and raises an eyebrow at me. "Is that so?"

I flick my brother in the temple, making a mockery of the pest he is. "That's not true at all. This scoundrel is just trying to win you over. Don't let him. He's a slob and a terrible mouth breather. I had to share a room with him until I was fifteen."

Burton flips me his middle finger, which Mom sees, and she

promptly whacks him on the head with her sauce spoon. It leaves a trail of red in his light brown locks, and he starts whining, running off to the bathroom.

"Smith," Mom greets me, pressing up on her toes and expecting me to lean down and kiss her cheek.

I do so, because I respect the hell out of my mom, and then introduce Molly. "Mom, this is Molly. I don't know if you remember her—"

"Justin's ex-girlfriend, of course I do." Mom gives my girlfriend the hawk-eye, and I'm so apprehensive, I might break a tooth I'm grinding down so hard on my molars.

It's vitally important that my family not only like Molly, but accept her. It's rare that I bring a girl home to any family function, for that matter, and this isn't just any woman. This is *the* woman.

"Then again, you were way too good for him. We all saw it. And what that schmuck did to you, and to my best friend, his mother? He never deserved you." Mom points her sauce spoon at us. "My son is a much better man, I hope you understand how genuine and special he is."

"Ma ..." I start to scold her, but Molly interrupts me.

"Believe me, I'm well aware of Smith's character. He's a wonderful, caring man, Mrs. Redfield. You did an amazing job, with all of your children. I really admire that."

My mother nods her head as if what Molly is saying is fact. "Well, I've heard about some of the wonderful things you've done for the youth of our city. I'd like to talk to you about that."

"Anytime." Molly smiles triumphantly, as if she passed some kind of test to be accepted into my family.

"Good, wash your hands and grab a chair. Those meatballs aren't going to roll themselves, and I have to show you the family recipe. We can talk while we work." Mom points at one of our old, wooden kitchen chairs.

I snort, because she may have passed the first test, but Molly is about to get initiated. Her face is pleasantly surprised as she turns to me, and I shrug, knowing I will never rescue her from this duty.

"I'll be in the living room with the men." I hike a thumb toward the doorway.

I leave the two of them in the kitchen, glancing back to see that they're deep in conversation. There is shouting in the living room, and no doubt Dad has the baseball game on. I wander in to see my dad, his brother Jack, my sister Katrina and my two nephews Chase and Clinton watching the Mets on TV, and Harrison and Erica standing off to the side.

"Smith!" The two seven-year-old twins jump up and wrap themselves around my waste.

"Hey, ya rascals." I ruffle their dark black hair. "What's the score?"

"Two zero, Mets." Dad waves distractedly in greeting.

"You know not to talk to him during a game. He's rubbing off on the boys." Katrina smirks and rolls her eyes as I bend down to kiss her cheek.

I nod to my uncle, who nods back but is too engrossed in the game, then head over to talk to Erica and Harrison. I haven't talked to Harrison much since the blowup at restaurant depot, and things have been strained. Neither he nor I have taken the initiative to solve it, but I should man up and be the bigger man. I was the one who blew up, who stormed out. I've seen, through a lot of conversations with Molly, how much my grief has manifested itself in the wrong ways, and even if I couldn't move as quickly as my family through the stages, I needed to give them a little proof of my healing.

"Hey," I say to both my brother and my sister as I approach them.

Erica leans in for a side hug, and Harrison just nods, obviously still miffed about what went down between us.

"Molly here?" Erica asks.

My whole family has been dying to meet her. Some of them already have back when she was with Justin, but this is different. We're together now, and my family knows I don't get involved seriously with someone if they don't have my whole heart. Probably because I've never really *been* involved with someone. The fact I brought her here says a lot.

"Yeah, she's in the kitchen with Ma," I confirm.

"Ah, getting grilled about her upbringing and intentions, I suppose." Erica snorts.

We all know the drill when it comes to our mother.

"She'll do fine. She's an angel," Harrison chimes in.

He spent some time with Molly while she was with Justin and even voiced to me how wrong he thought my best friend was for her. That she was too good for our childhood buddy.

An awkward silence descends on our little group as I don't respond, and Erica pipes up, "I'm gonna, uh ... get something to drink."

She makes a hasty exit, leaving us conveniently alone to talk. My siblings were never subtle, and I'm sure they've all heard about my blow up at the restaurant depot.

"How you been, Smith?" Harrison asks, starting the conversation.

"Pretty good, actually. Been spending a lot of time with Molly, and when we're not in the Hamptons, I'm at the new restaurant. Or the old ones, but those are well-oiled machines."

He nods slowly, and I think he might just continue this small talk, but my oldest brother jumps right into it. "Was expecting a call or an apology from you, but I guess you couldn't find the time."

I roll my eyes at his melodrama. "Stop it, don't take that passive aggressive tone with me."

"What? I just would have loved an explanation for getting stormed out on in the middle of a department store." He shrugs as if he's innocent.

"Harrison, you pushed me too far, and you know it. It wasn't the time or the place for that conversation, at least admit that. I know I'm at fault too, I overreacted. I'm sorry about that, I shouldn't have flown off the handle."

My brother, ever the stubborn one, crosses his arms over his chest. "Fine, so maybe I didn't need to prod you that hard. I'm sorry about that."

At least we've both uttered the words now, no matter how begrudgingly.

"Can you just respect that I'm handling things in my own way, in my own time? I've been killing myself at the restaurant, and that's my monument to Stephanie. Let me grieve in the way I need to."

Harrison chews this over, and then nods. "She is really changing you. Or at least, you've found someone who is finally helping you to talk about Steph's death. I'm thankful for that."

A weight moves off my chest, because it seems that the tension and apologies have been cleared or spoken between us. He's talking about Molly, and while I haven't told my family so much, he's not wrong in his assumptions.

"She has. She's ... well ..."

Harrison lays a hand on my arm. "You don't have to put words to it, trust me, I get it. It was the same for me when I met Kenneth."

My head simply bobs at the comparison, because he knows. Anyone who has met the human who feels like the other half of their soul understands.

That's what Molly is for me.

32

MOLLY

Smith introduced me to his family, and so it was only natural that I'd want him to meet mine.

I waited for a weekend that my parents had free and then scheduled a lunch at their house, making it completely convenient for them. I wouldn't dare to ask them to come out to our beautiful house in the Hamptons, because Lord knows they never would have. My parents don't venture from their NJ suburb, nor do they agree with the lifestyle of those in the Hamptons.

And I secretly want Smith to see where I grew up. Meeting his enormous family opened my eyes to exactly who Smith is, though I was getting the whole picture way before then. It gave me insight into how his brain works, what he holds important, and I want him to see the same. Back when he was teasing and taunting me, Smith made so many comments about my underprivileged upbringing. He would pick on me for being a simpleton, for being too sweet or naive.

Maybe I am. Maybe I'm a hometown girl who happened to move to the city, and it hasn't quite seeped into my blood. But I want him to see where I came from, why I wasn't like a lot of the other women he hung around with.

"Welcome to Linden." I smile as he parks his car in my parent's driveway.

"Hm, looks like New Jersey." He sticks his tongue out at me.

We've had this debate numerous times over the past few weeks, of which is better, New York or New Jersey? Obviously, we each take a side, and no one agrees at the end. It usually gets solved with Smith kissing me, distracting me, and then we're not even talking anymore. He's *really* good at that.

"And what is that supposed to mean?" My eyebrows crease, I can feel it.

"Oh, *nothing*," he singsongs and unfolds himself from the car.

"Okay, so no talk of money, even if they bring it up. And no talk of living in the room next door to mine at the beach house, Dad won't like that. Definitely don't mention we're sleeping together, and if they ask, say you're in restaurants. Don't tell them that you own them."

I lay out these instructions as we walk up to my parent's front door, a bottle of wine in my hand and a bouquet of flowers for my mother in Smith's arms.

Smith nods. "Got it. I'll throw a wad of cash on the table, ask them if they've rented any private jets recently, and then tell your parents I'm going down on their daughter nightly."

His sarcasm has me laughing, a nervous jitter that works its way out of my throat. "You're horrible."

"And you need to relax. I know how to be a human being, Molly." He rolls his eyes.

I know he does, I've seen it plenty of times. Smith can be extremely charming when the situation calls for it. But I know my parents. They're going to look at his styled jeans and T-shirt that cost more than a trip to the movies, an expense for them, and judge him right off the bat.

And I really like this guy. I'm falling for him more each day. Looking back on my time with Justin, I thought I'd been doing the same thing, but now I know better. This was what it is supposed to feel like when you meet your soul mate, even if he pretended to hate you for a year.

My fist knocks once on the screen door before I unlatch it and let myself in. "Mom? We're here!"

The announcement is met by some shuffling in the kitchen, and then out she walks, red checkered apron tightly secured around her waist.

"Hi, honey. You made good time?" She comes over to hug me.

"We did." I hug her back.

I'm acutely aware of how quiet it is here as opposed to Smith's house, and I kind of miss the chaos. Going to his parent's home was a surprise around every corner, a new conversation every second, and so much love. My parents and I made the best of our little unit, but I missed something I never knew I was missing ever since I'd spent time with the Redfields.

"Mom, this is Smith." I step back, waving my hand at the tall, stunning man standing next to me.

Mom sticks out her hand, and I can already tell her demeanor is apprehensive. *Crap.*

"Smith, nice to meet you." She shakes his hand, and it's forced and weird.

"Mrs. Archer, I've heard so many wonderful things about you." He shakes her hand and then offers the flowers he brought.

"Well, these are beautiful. I'll get them in some water." She scurries to the kitchen, and I should have known from the start that this was how the rest of the day would go.

We find Dad in his shop out back, and he's just as brisk with his greeting of Smith. I know they've already had a little powwow, and decided they weren't even going to entertain the idea of warming to my boyfriend.

Lunch is awkward at best, and frigid at worst. My parents barely speak when spoken to, no matter how hard Smith turns on the charm. I try my hardest to run around the conversation like a show dog, bringing up points and making everyone sparkle. But it does no good; my parents want nothing to do with him.

Mom is washing the dishes in the kitchen after, and I approach her cautiously, sitting down at our small kitchen table.

"Smith's pretty great, huh?" I start, baiting her.

The buzz of annoyance is holding me in its grasp, because I wanted to show Smith how wonderful my family is. Just like he'd shown me, and I wanted the connection I found in Queens to translate here to my hometown. But my parents have been obstinate and cold, and I am honestly not only embarrassed, but sad that we'd have to overcome their prejudiced opinions.

"Hmm ..." She clucks her tongue, and my temper flares.

"What is it? Just say it. I'm not an idiot, Mom." I sound like the petulant teenager I never was, but I can't help it.

"First, a banker, and now a man who owns restaurants? Jeez, Molly girl, you really developed some expensive boyfriend tastes when you moved to the city."

Mom's words barb and twist around my heart. They hurt more because my parents know my character, but can't see past their own insecurities and tainted history with people of a higher salary band. I'm so fed up with that kind of attitude, but I'm even more pissed off that this is all she sees Smith as.

My blood is boiling as I address her back where she's washing the dishes in the sink.

"For your information, both of those men grew up in a very

lower middle-class neighborhood in Queens. Smith is one of eight children, and his mother and father worked every day to provide those kids with food and a roof over their heads. Yes, Justin was a piece of crap. He boasted about his money and threw around the newfound privilege he'd earned. I'll give you that. But aside from the way he broke up with me, he was never anything but kind to your daughter, and you. You should remember that. As for Smith, he's one of the most hardworking people I've ever encountered. You know he never went to college, just like Dad? He worked as a dishwasher in restaurants until he could learn enough and work his way up to a more prominent position. And then when the option came along to not work for someone else anymore, he did most of the construction on his first eatery. He only has one other partner, and they work just as hard if not harder as you and me. You have no idea the kind of man he is, but you're judging him based on his income. Which he's worked like a dog for. Not that you'd know he's worth that much, since he's one of the kindest, and most understanding humans I've ever encountered. You would know, if you bothered to ask him anything about himself, that he still takes his mother to church on Sundays and volunteers at his niece's ballet recital to work the bake sale table. Just because someone has money doesn't make them a villain, and I'm sick of you and Dad treating people that way."

I'm so heated that I stand up, sending the kitchen chair flying, and stomp out of the kitchen entryway. But I only get four steps before smashing right into Smith's chest. With just a look up into those stormy indigo eyes, I can tell he heard every word. He practically hauls me up by the waist, until my feet are barely skimming the floor, and holds me to him while he smashes his mouth to mine.

The kiss is scorching, branding me from the inside out, and we're fully making out in my childhood home hallway within three seconds. His large, steel erection presses into my belly, and I'm clinging to his neck for dear life. A hurricane swirls low in my core, and I'm needy within the minute.

"Jeanie?" The screen door slams and my dad's footsteps echo through the front hall. "Have you seen my tire pressure gauge?"

Smith sets me down, my back pressing against the wall, as we suck in lungfuls of breaths, our eyes frantically trying to focus on each other because we're so close.

"Let's get out of here," I whisper.

"I love you," he answers.

Right there, in the small hallway of my childhood house, standing on the red shag carpeting, Smith Redfield told me he loves me. A sensation runs through my chest, smooth and languid as a river. It's one of absolute knowing, that this is the man I've waited for to say those words. Others have said them before, but it's like the universe clicked into perfect view when Smith said them.

I grab ahold of his hand, heading straight for my parent's front door.

"Where are you off to?" Dad asks, but I brush right past him.

Not only am I furious at my parents for disrespecting Smith, but I'm mad at them for not trusting my judgment. They raised me better than that, and their prejudice against others for wanting a better life for themselves or living a different lifestyle was honestly on my last nerve.

I'll call later and apologize for storming out, but right now, I want to get back to my little world with Smith.

He just told me he's in love with me, and I need not only the right moment to tell him, but the right actions to show him.

Because I knew before this day, but now I'm sure.

I am in love with this man, and it's deeper and more intense than any love I've ever experienced, or any I'll experience from this point forward.

33

SMITH

August twentieth is a day I've been dreading since January.

Normally, I'd be sharing this day with Stephanie, but obviously that wasn't happening this year. For thirty years, we'd shared a birthday, joined as a pair since birth, and now that tradition would be no more.

As if this day isn't going to be shitty enough, it's also the second to last weekend in the Hampton's house. Next weekend, we'll have to pack this place up and head back to our permanent dwellings in the city to wait for the winter months to close in. The weight of it all seems to be slowly crushing me, like an anvil in slow motion.

I don't want this summer to end. While this year has been hell, these last three months have been a saving grace. They've brought me a love I thought I'd never be able to have, and being in such a beautiful place while it blossomed didn't hurt either. Now Molly and I would be thrust back into the chaos of Manhattan, of full-time jobs, and the pressure of the East Coast grind. I wasn't worried about how our relationship would thrive, but it would mean seeing less of each other, which already had me wanting to climb the walls.

Not that I was extremely pleased with her right now.

"Come dance with me." Molly tugs on my hand, her blond ponytail slicked back off her face.

I can see every thick eyelash accentuated by her makeup, and her body is a wet dream encased in that blush pink silk dress.

But I can't seem to bring myself to feel anything. Arousal, bittersweet contentment, happiness. Actually, that's not true. I feel something. I feel furious.

Molly has been pushing and pushing all night, whether she realizes it or not. The pushing started about a week ago, when she started asking me what I wanted to do for my birthday. I could barely stomach to talk about the subject and told her that I didn't even want to celebrate. She'd tilt her head in sympathy and nod her understanding, but then say something like, "but we should make good, new memories on this day."

Did she not understand? I wanted to make no kind of memories on this day. I wanted to down five fingers of whiskey and go to sleep.

Instead, here I am at a crowded, loud lounge after suffering through a dinner at what is usually my favorite restaurant in the Hamptons. I couldn't even taste the food, that's how annoyed I was.

"No, I don't want to dance." I all but smack her hand away, picking up my drink and downing the burning, amber liquid instead.

At least I could get drunk, though the more I consume, the more rage builds up in my veins.

"Smith." She looks both shocked and hurt that I would so blatantly rebuff her.

What does she expect? I've told her how hard Stephanie's

death has been on me. I told her about my bad days, even let her in on one when we went to the cliffs above the beach together.

I also told her I love her. I heard her defend me, and my heart had nearly exploded. She stood up to her own mother to save my name, to prove that I am a good man. It was what I was hoping she'd see in me all along, and I couldn't hold back the words any longer.

But Molly hasn't given them to me, yet. I know it has only been two months since we started dating, but I know that she knows this is more than anything she felt with previous men. Which pisses me off even more. Here I am, sitting at a bar that I didn't want to be at, on a day I didn't want to celebrate, with a woman I thought knew me better than anyone, but apparently, she doesn't.

And she couldn't even say I love you back.

"You know what? I'm fucking out of here." I stand, knocking over the chair as I do, and don't bother to pick it up.

I'm belligerent and ticked off, and I know I'm blowing up, but I'm not unjustified. She claims to really care about me, but will she ever care about me the way I do about her? Fuck, I pined silently after this woman for a year.

Stomping out of the bar, I make my way to the parking lot, anger buzzing in my blood like poison.

"Hey, wait!" Molly is coming after me, something I expected.

I swing around, my fuse blowing at the exact worst time. "No, I won't wait. I won't sit through another goddamn minute of your 'new fucking memories' because I don't want to make them! You ever stop to consider how I might feel today, or were you just concerned with being the perfect little girlfriend?"

Molly rears back, pain flashing in her hazel eyes. "Smith, I didn't ... oh gosh, I'm so sorry. I should have known. I thought maybe if I just kept ..."

"Yeah, you sure thought that, huh?" I didn't even let her get her thought out, but rational argument is out the window for me. "But you didn't actually listen to me. You've never actually listened to me. Or seen me, apparently."

I'm practically shouting at her, but everyone here is drunk. Or maybe I'm too drunk and grieving to care if all these other people hear our fight.

"That's not true at all. This summer has been the best time of my life, all because of you. I just wanted to show you that tonight." Her cheeks are turning a shade of pink that means she's upset.

"By dragging me out to every place I didn't want to be today? I thought you knew me better than that. But then, I forget you spent the first year of us knowing each other in my best friend's bed. Maybe you're confusing me with him."

It's a low blow, and it's pathetic that it feels so good.

Hurt and fury mix in her expression, and I hear the unshed tears in her throat when she responds to me. "Smith, how dare you say—"

But I cut her off. "I was in love with you from the very first fucking time I saw you! Justin tapped me on the shoulder the night he first brought you to meet us, I turned around, and there you fucking were. Standing there as if I hadn't waited my entire life up until that moment searching for you, and I didn't even know I'd been searching. And you looked at me with ... *nothing*. Nothing but a polite smile as you held my best friend's hand, and then went home to fuck him the same night every star in the universe aligned for me. I waited, I waited for what felt like an eternity, Molly, for you to notice me. And then, by some miracle, you did. Except you still don't feel the way I do about you. I told you I'm in love with you, and you couldn't even say it back!"

"That's not fair. You shouldn't want me to say it back just because you expressed your feelings to me. I need my own time to do that." Molly's voice breaks, and I can hear the pleading in it.

"So, you don't love me?" I'm not sure how I started picking on this bone, but I'm here.

"You're not really mad over this. Don't make this something it's not. I understand you're upset about your birthday, and I'm sorry I was insensitive of that. But don't ruin this," Molly warns, her voice trembling.

"We were doomed from the start." The finality in my voice has me wanting to punch myself, but I can't stop this ball of hate and self-destruction that I have rolling.

"Don't say that," Molly whispers, wringing her hands.

"Wasn't it easier hating me? Wasn't it easier pretending I was an asshole? Because then you wouldn't have to pretend to try to love me when I confessed those feelings to you?"

This is the crux of my issue, the thing that will always stand between us. I was a jerk to her for months, and she was okay with it because she was with him. She was with *him*.

"None of this is true, Smith." A tear slips down her cheek, and now I've made her cry.

This day couldn't get any worse. And not only am I heartbroken and pissed off, but now I'm exhausted, too.

I walk off, not bothering to add any more fuel to the dumpster fire I started. Maybe I'll call a cab. Maybe I'll just walk all the way home.

It'll be punishment, and the perfect ending to this fucking awful day.

34

MOLLY

Waking up this morning, the pounding in my head is worse than any hangover I've ever had.

I barely slept, drifting into a fitful, restless sleep sometime in the night because my body must have figured it needed to do it for my heart's sake. After Smith had chewed me out, I'd called my own cab and came back to the summer house with Marta and Ray, who decided not to let me leave on my own. Hiding in my room felt like the safe bet, waiting for the inevitable storm to pick back up when Smith returned to the house.

But he never came. I curled against my pillows, crying like a dramatic soap opera heroine, for what felt like hours. It had been a bad choice to celebrate his birthday, and I'd been the one to push him into it. I thought that if we made happy memories, if I could put on my best cheerful face, that it would make him forget that his sister wasn't here.

Of course, he wasn't going to forget that. It was his first birthday after his twin had all but been murdered, and I was a naive fool to think it would go any other way.

While I waited for Smith to get home, I cried for him. I cried for the pain he must be in today, for the broken man who confessed all of those deep, buried feelings for me. He'd watched me fall in love with another man for more than a year. And not just any other man, but his best friend. And he stood by and respected that. It spoke volumes about who he is as a person.

But I also cried for me. For the ugly words that were flung at me, for the messed-up situation I'd gotten myself into. I hate that I hadn't seen what was right in front of me, that I'd been so wrapped up in the pomp and circumstance of Justin that I hadn't seen the better man waiting for me.

I cried because I wanted to tell Smith I am in love with him, but was scared that it was too fast after my breakup with Justin. I should have just said the words, they're in my heart so clearly, but I hadn't. And I wasn't going to say them as an answer to some ultimatum.

When he finally got home, it was close to two a.m. I was awake, but exhausted from crying, and he never even approached my door. I heard him move swiftly past it, heard his lock click, and then the house fell silent. He wasn't coming.

I don't know where we go from here. I was in the wrong for wanting to celebrate; it was insensitive and I needed to apologize for it. I knew Smith better than that, and should have shown him my support yesterday.

But the accusations and insults he hurled yesterday were ones that couldn't be taken back. I don't even know if we're together anymore, with the way we left things. That sounds dramatic, but there was this clear hurdle he couldn't get over when it came to me and my past with his best friend, and I'm not sure I can ever repair that mental block for him.

My fingers twist the laces of my sneakers as the sadness sits heavy on my heart and shoulders. Heather came to my room this morning and convinced me to get out, that a bit of fresh air and exercise would be therapeutic. It was better than sitting in my bedroom and crying, so I agreed. Plus, I couldn't sit in here when I knew Smith was occupying another space in the house, not wanting to or not able to come apologize.

I meet Heather and Jacinda out on the driveway after grabbing a granola bar for breakfast. I barely taste it as I wash it down with a gulp of water, but I know subconsciously that I need fuel for this ride.

We are about to depart, our feet practically on the pedals of the bikes ready to start, when a cab pulls down the driveway.

"Who is that?" Heather wonders aloud, because everyone else is home.

And even though he hasn't come to see or talk to me, I know Smith is in his room. I heard him shuffling around in there as I tiptoed down the stairs. Because believe me, if this was Smith getting out of a cab after a night sleeping out somewhere, I would be devastated.

But no. My heart drops, shattering on the driveway, for a completely different reason.

"Just the girls I wanted to see!"

Closing the door of the cab, with his arms stretched wide in that cocky, welcoming gesture he always liked to assume, is my ex-boyfriend. Justin is standing on the driveway of our summer house, in a three-piece suit and shining cognac loafers.

His hair is gelled back to within an inch of its life, I can see the sparkle of the Rolex he constantly brags about on his wrist, and he's sporting a tan that definitely looks sprayed on. Now that I'm looking at him, his blond hair gleaming with the highlights he puts in it, and his beakish nose too angled and snobby, I have no idea what I ever saw in the guy.

Smith might be a polished businessman, but he still had that down-to-earth nature about him. He looked just as at-home in sweatpants as he did in a suit, and wore them instead of the clothing wearing him.

Observing Justin now, I find that there is no pull of attraction. My heart doesn't flip-flop when I see him, I don't have any desire to run back to him. There is no angst in my soul remembering what we had.

"What are you doing here?" The tone of Jacinda's voice is unreadable, but she does dismount her bike and walk over to him, giving him a hug.

"I had to close a deal in New York for my new company, and I figured that I'd come out here and surprise you guys! Hey, Heather." He waves to my best friend as he hugs Jacinda close.

Heather is not anywhere close to amused. "Um, why did you think it would be a good idea to come out here? None of your friends, or you girlfriend for that matter, have heard from you since you abandoned them four months ago."

Well, she certainly wasn't going for subtlety.

But Justin just laughs it off, his hearty, rich chuckle sounding way more fake than I remember it being. "Wow, wasn't the welcome I was expecting but guess it was the one I deserve."

He walks closer, and my heart does nothing. This is not the man it belongs to now. The one who has it is upstairs, our relationship in the balance, and I can't be anything but annoyed at the sight of my ex.

"Mol, you look beautiful." Justin's green eyes take me in, and he lowers his voice. "I owe you a big apology, and I'm hoping we can talk while I'm here."

He's offering something I've waited months for, and now that he's standing in front of me, I realize I no longer need the closure. What he did was messed up, it broke my heart for a time, and I used to think I had so many questions. But now that Justin was able to give them, I realize I don't really care what the explanations are. They'll most likely be lies anyway, and I no longer need his words to put that chapter of my life to bed.

What I do need is the open road and some quiet time for my brain to process what happened last night, and how I can move forward.

"Maybe later. We're going for a bike ride." I put my feet on the pedals and nod to my friends.

I don't miss the way my ex-boyfriend's jaw drops a little when I so coolly reject his olive branch. He's not used to that, at all, and his ego will never let him admit that I'm right in doing so.

But I will say it feels satisfyingly good to stand up for myself, even if this wasn't the man I wanted attention from.

35

SMITH

Justin is sitting in the living room of our rental house, the one he procured, shooting the shit with our other friends.

I'm upstairs currently pacing my bedroom floor, wondering what the hell I do now or how I should act. On the one hand, I'm glad my best friend is back for a visit. In a peripheral way, I've missed him, because he's been around for most of my life. On another level, I'm absolutely pissed he ghosted us for months without warning, and I'm angry that he left at such a vulnerable time for me right after I lost Stephanie.

And then on a completely other level, I don't want him here at all. He's Molly's ex-boyfriend, which by default means I don't want him anywhere in the picture. If he was any other random ex, I'd be annoyed to be in his presence. But I'm even more so now, because I had the agony of watching their entire relationship unfold. I've seen him kiss her, heard about their fights from him, and heard him treat her terribly even when they were together.

I know I have to go down there, it's weird I haven't greeted him yet, but when Marta came up to tell me, I panicked even more. This timing couldn't be worse, what with everything that happened with Molly last night. Oh, and I'd gotten a damn good earful of Marta's opinion when she dropped the Justin bomb, too.

The minute I walk out of my door into the hallway, Peter is there.

"So, am I keeping my mouth shut about you and Molly, then?" he whispers, genuinely looking concerned and confused.

I know he's asking out of support, because he likes us together. But he's also probably worried about our other best friend, though the guy didn't bother cluing us in when he moved halfway across the world.

And honestly, at this point, what is there to tell? Molly and I haven't spoken all day, I screamed at her on my birthday, and now her ex-boyfriend is here.

The two of them have such unresolved business, I'm not sure where I fit. Would she go back to him if he begged her? The thought of that makes me want to punch a wall or maybe my best friend's snooty, spray-tanned face. I always hated that he went and got those fake things, it makes him even prissier than he already is.

"Yeah. Don't mention it. Honestly, after last night, who knows if we're even together anymore." I bury my face in my hands.

"Well, you would know, if you manned up and talked to her. Dude, you claim that you spent the better part of a year pining over her, and now you have the chance to win her back when Justin shows up and you're just going to squander that? I thought more of you, brother. You love her, we all know it. Don't let that go because you're salty and grieving. We both know Molly did nothing wrong, and that she was only trying to help. Get your head out of your ass and let someone in. You won't do it for me, you won't do it for your family, but don't you lose her. You'll be kicking yourself for a lifetime."

His unexpected diatribe feels like a swift jab in the throat. "Jesus, I didn't realize this was an intervention."

Peter smirks. "I only give them when one of my very best friends is being a stubborn asshole, which you are."

I rub at my temples, exhausted by the whole thing. "I know, I just ... it's been a tough week with Steph and everything."

"The fact that your sister isn't here on your shared birthday has nothing to do with the woman you're in love with. And are possibly about to lose. You want her? Go fight for her. Don't let that slimy, Singapore son-of-a-bitch get her back."

He's right, and those words of encouragement are exactly what I need to march downstairs.

Except, when I get to the living room, neither Molly nor Justin are sitting with the rest of the housemates.

"Where is Molly?" I ask them, and every eye in the room swings to me.

Heather looks fucking pissed, so clearly she isn't going to tell me. Jacinda's eyes flit away a second later, pretending to be oblivious. She loves both Justin and me, and I don't blame her for not wanting to get involved.

It's Marta who finally speaks, frustration and a little bit of smugness in her tone. "She and Justin took a walk. They're talking."

I know what my sister's best friend is trying to do. She's told me for a year that I should confess my feelings for Molly, and now that I fucked things up last night, she thinks I'm getting the medicine I deserve.

Maybe I am. But it doesn't hurt like a bitch any less.

"Where did they go?" I ask.

"Down the beach," she responds.

They're talking, obviously, about their relationship and how he screwed up. Will she tell him we've been seeing each other? Will she tell him what she feels for me? I don't even know her true feelings, so it's naive to think she'll stand on that hill in front of her ex-boyfriend.

My heart feels like a dead, leaden thing sitting inside my chest. I slump down on the couch, knowing that I should have apologized before this and now possibly won't have the chance.

I said things last night that hurt Molly to her core, things that weren't true and were unfair to ask of someone. I let my own anger blind me, and for the first time, was seeing how much the grief I wasn't dealing with was hurting everyone around me.

I could lose her. I could be losing her right this moment.

That thought crushes me, and I honestly don't know how I'll survive if she decides to go back to him.

I did it once, and it turned me into a hateful, spiteful person. Would I have to go back to that guy?

If Molly told me she loved Justin, and that she was giving him a second chance, I'd have no choice. Turning my heart black would be the only option.

36

MOLLY

"This is so depressing."

Marta shuts another cabinet door, sulking as she places a few boxes of crackers into the large shopping bags of food we're taking home with us.

"Tell me about it. It feels like the summer just started. I can't believe we have to leave." Heather pretends to wipe away a fake tear, but she's really half-joking.

I think we're all feeling it today, since it's our last day in the Hampton's house. The bedrooms have been packed up, drawers emptied, suitcases placed in the trunks of cars. The pool floats have been deflated, and the random paperbacks we've been scattering around the living room all summer have been boxed up. Now the girls and I are working on the kitchen, while the men take the beach chairs, umbrellas, and other items on the sand back to the storage space in the garage.

"It was a wonderful summer." Jacinda sighs, and we all know she means it more than anyone.

This is the place where she got engaged, the place where we started to talk about her and Peter's wedding. It's been a summer to remember.

But for me, I'm a little relieved it's coming to a close. When this house share started, I felt like the outsider. I wasn't even sure I should come, and I was nursing both a broken heart and battered ego. Over the last few months, I've really blossomed in this group. And outside of what happened with Smith, I'm happy to say that I've made some lifelong friends. Not only that, but for the first time in my adult life, I gave myself permission to relax. To take a break. One that I didn't even really realize I needed until I was doing it.

It's bittersweet, the summer coming to an end, because it was a great few months. But I can't ignore that being in this house any longer would only deepen my hurt, that it would only crush my heart more with each passing day. Smith and I still haven't spoken about the night of his birthday, both of our own stubbornness preventing it.

I should have apologized by now, about not respecting his wishes, but I think what he accused me of is worse. And Jacinda let slip that Smith told Peter he thought I was back together with Justin after my ex's surprise visit. He's been avoiding me like the plague, and the fact that he thinks I'd abandon him that easily shows just what he thinks of me as a person.

My conversation with Justin was awkward, and I can't say much else to describe it. He tried to apologize profusely, turning on the sympathy valve as if I was ever going to understand his logic in hiding his move for months and then breaking up with me as he sat on the tarmac. *Via text.* He bullshitted about commitment issues and feeling too settled, but realized he threw it all away just days into getting to Singapore.

When I asked why he never called if he felt that way, he lied some more, throwing out cliché excuse after cliché excuse that aren't even worth repeating. Justin never truly took accountability for breaking my heart, for leaving me with no explanation, and for ruining the life we were building together.

As I sat there listening to him drone on about how incredible his apartment in Singapore is, how much money he was making, and how I should come out and visit him, I couldn't help but think that I truly never knew this person. Maybe I thought I had, but he'd fooled me. His heart was never mine, and now that I knew what true love looks like, I could never go back to something like that. Not that Justin hadn't asked; he'd practically gotten down on his knees on the beach and asked if we could give things a second shot. I have no idea why he asked, because he made his life and dating potential across the world sound like a dream, but maybe it was seeing me happy. He had no idea that I was with Smith, if I was even still with Smith, but I reckon that would have only served to make him want me back more. Justin is a game player, someone who likes what he can't grasp in the moment, and I was done being his pawn. Had been done a long time ago.

I told him no, that he hurt me to my core, but that I no longer felt anything for him. I didn't make the "I'm seeing someone" excuse or ramble about how he broke my heart, I held my head high and refused him for all the things he'd done. I didn't need to come up with reasons why I wasn't available; I was simply not available because he didn't deserve to be in a relationship with me.

The walk back had been brutally silent, and he sulked the entire night he stayed with us at the beach house. He and the boys went out that night, and I have no idea if Smith told him about us or not, but I didn't see Justin the next morning. I haven't heard from him since, and I'm assuming he crawled back to the airplane he came from. Good riddance, and I'm glad I can say that I've finally closed that chapter.

The French doors open and the men come back into the kitchen. Peter catches Jacinda's attention, and they walk out, heading for the beach. Ray pulls Marta in another direction, and when I finally pick my head up, Heather has gone off somewhere as well. It's just Smith and me, left in our tension-filled bubble.

"Ready to leave your keys?" he asks, that deep voice sending a pang of loneliness through me.

I spent most of last week in the city, preparing my classroom, and trying not to see him. It hurts to even look at him, knowing what we had before the disaster of his birthday.

"Yes," I say simply, my eyes cast down as I pretend to look through the shopping bags of leftover food.

"It was a good summer." I feel Smith's pull, the magnetic energy between us strong.

I miss lying in his arms; I miss him kissing me awake in the morning. I miss the way he looks at me as if I'm the only other person in the room.

"It was," I agree, unsure of what to say.

Is that what he's doing, saying goodbye? We had a nice summer fling, but once the door to this house is shut, any possibility between us is gone, too? I want to scream in frustration, or berate him for the things he said to me, but the good girl in me keeps quiet. I won't make myself look like a fool if what we had isn't something he even cares about.

"Molly ..." Smith trails off, and there are so many words left unsaid.

I take a deep breath, knowing I have to get one thing off my chest, before I never see him again. Who knows after this, if we'll ever be in the same room together. Smith has no reason to see me after we leave the Hamptons.

"I'm sorry about your birthday. I shouldn't have pushed you, and it was not considerate at all to cast your pain and grief aside. I apologize for any hurt I caused you that day."

There. My conscience is clear. Anything I felt guilty about was now off my shoulders.

Looking up, I'm met with a desperate blue gaze. "Tell me you're not with him?"

That's what he cares about, me and Justin? He could have said so many things just now, and he chose the jealousy inside his head.

My expression shuts down, my heart turning to dust. "No, I didn't get back together with Justin. But the fact that it's the first thing on your mind, the only thing of concern, is really telling. You're more worried about this competition you have with your friend, rather than the love you say you have for me. Someone who loves another person doesn't say the things you did the other night. And they don't leave them hanging, without explanation, without apology. This was never about who I was going to choose. I chose you, from the minute I stepped foot in this house. Before I even realized it was you I was meant to be with. Once you kissed me, I never thought of anyone else. But you're fueled by this envy, and you act on rage. I deserve better than that."

I don't raise my voice, and I don't cry. For those two things, I'm thankful that I could keep my composure. I take out my keys, pulling the one to the front door of this house off.

Smith watches as I place it gently on the kitchen counter.

Neither of us says anything more, and ten minutes later, I'm looking out the window of Heather's rental as we drive out of the Hamptons for good.

37

MOLLY

If you looked up the definition of what my September always looks like in the dictionary, you would find it under hectic.

The beginning of school always seems to happen with a poof of chaos, a lot of learning curves, and too many sleepless nights. There are lesson plans to tweak, students to get reined in, administrators to bargain with, and the lackluster parents who don't seem to care if their children show up for school or not.

On top of all of my work as a teacher, I still pick up shifts at Aja. Because the beginning of the school year is so crazy, it means I often underestimate the supplies and books my students will need. Sometimes, I have to buy one or more of them backpacks because they show up without them. Other times, I'll find out that one of my students isn't eating during the day because they can't even afford the subsidized meal plan. I need the extra cash, but the extra work hours are brutal on my exhaustion.

It's worth it, though, to see my students safe and healthy. By the end of October, things should even out. It just feels like I'm a hamster running on a loop right now.

I did happen to get a rare Sunday off and decided to make the trek to New Jersey since my parents have been bugging me about coming by.

The scent of Dad cooking his famous ribs invades my nose, and I'm almost drooling.

"Honey, did you get serving utensils for the potato and pasta salad?" Mom asks, carrying two large bowls as she exits the back screen door.

I stand, moving to take one from her. "I did, they're on the table."

We set the dishes down together, and then sit, her nursing a glass of wine and me an iced tea. It's like old times, the three of us grilling on a Sunday afternoon, and I know that Dad will turn the football game up on the radio as soon as we sit down to eat.

"How is school going?" Mom asks, genuinely curious.

I get my gene for teaching from her, and she's one of the best educators I know. She's tough but compassionate and goes above and beyond to help her students succeed. She's the kind of teacher I emulate.

"It's going, all right. My students this year are good ones, but per usual, they need a ton of help and support. I say it every year, but I can't believe the way the system lets these kids fall through the cracks. I can't believe some of the parents who don't even care if their children flunk out of school, much less show up."

Mom nods in agreement, as if she's seen this too many times to count. "It's a crappy world sometimes, Mol, but that's why we keep going back. Someone has to help them, look after them. I'm proud of you, it isn't an easy task."

She pats me on the hand and takes another sip of wine. Dad comes over with a plate full of saucy, dripping barbecue ribs, and I have to restrain myself from digging in. It's not often that someone cooks for me these days, and the comfort of being taken care of by your parents is one that still soothes the soul even into your thirties.

"You still picking up shifts at the restaurant, too?" Dad asks as he sits down with us.

I nod, biting into my first rib. "Of course."

The conversation follows its normal pattern, of my parents checking in to see that I'm working myself like a dog. Then they transition to neighborhood gossip, followed by my father's favorite electrician stories of the week.

My parents don't know that Smith and I are no longer together. They weren't the biggest fans of him to begin with, and I don't need their snarky comments if I tell them we're not seeing each other. The reason we aren't together has nothing to do with Smith's money or his societal status, though that's what Mom and Dad would make it about.

I love my parents, but they are truly blinded from the background they come from. Instead of comforting their daughter over her breakup, it would be spitting on the names of rich people. I know that's how it would go. I'm so tired of being upset over this as it is, I don't need more judgment or anger where my love life is concerned.

I've still heard nothing from Smith, though I've had lunch with Jacinda once, and taken a spin class with Marta. I didn't ask about him, and they never brought him up. Part of me is grateful for that, because it means we have friendships based off something other than the men I'm dating within their circle. But the other half of me was desperate for any morsel of information, and when they didn't offer it, I felt slightly disappointed.

It's been almost three weeks since our fight, and two since we left the beach house. I don't regret what I said to him that final day, or how I left things, but I won't deny that I cry most nights.

The aching in my bones, the dry, hollowness of my eyes, the smashed up, fractured glass that is my heart ... they're a thousand times worse than any other breakup I've had. I miss him like crazy, and I keep hearing him tell me he loves me over and over in my dreams.

I want so badly to reach out to him, to be the one to break first, but I said my piece. I made my apology. And I don't deserve the way he treated me. If he ever cops to that, maybe it's a discussion we can have.

But I promised myself after Justin that I would never be that weak for a man ever again. And so I pick myself up every day, despite my broken heart, and try to hold my head high.

38

SMITH

Despite my restaurant having a fan-fucking-tastic soft opening last week for critics and chefs around Manhattan, I've been a miserable son of a bitch the last few weeks.

Whipping a restaurant into shape in time for an opening is a whole beast within itself, but add to it my horrible moods and pissed off attitude, and I've been a raging cloud of negativity looming over everyone's heads. I'm short with my family, my mother yelled at me the other day for missing a dinner, Campbell can't stand me and wants me to stop berating the new wait and kitchen staff. Peter told me I was a bastard the other day when I told him he was a fool to get married, and Justin and I are officially not on speaking terms since I wrote him an email in which I told him I was in love with Molly, and he was a moron for doing that to her. It was a chump move; I know that, doing it over email, but I couldn't bring myself to tell him in person. Not that we were really close any longer, after what he did leaving us all to move halfway across the world.

All in all, I was turning my life into a living hell, all because I couldn't man up and talk to the one person I needed to, to make things right.

I think about Molly night and day. I think about what I should say to her, and then my mind gets rolling, and the tangents just splinter off. Even in my own rehearsed speeches, I get defensive and cruel, and I'm not going to her until I can get my temper under control. She's fucking right, she deserves better than that.

Stefania's opening looming over my head is not helping; the pressure I feel to get this place right in every aspect to honor Steph is insurmountable. I feel a crushing weight on my shoulders every day, wanting to make every single detail perfect. While the soft opening went well, it wasn't with the full operation in swing, and that can always run off the rails quickly if not managed properly. While I have this much stress on me, I can do nothing but dig myself a deeper hole with Molly if I went to see her.

At least, that's what I'm telling myself. In reality, it's because I'm so in love with the woman that if she can't move past this, if I can't convince her to give me one last shot, I don't know what I'll do with myself. It's that catch twenty-two of wanting something so bad, but refraining because failure would be an even worse option.

The restaurant is buzzing with decorators, PR people, waiters, kitchen staff and some of our family members. It's officially the opening night of Stefania, and we're having a massive party to kick it off. All of Campbell and my nearest and dearest are attending, as well as industry professionals we know and some New York's finest restaurant critics.

I'm staring down at the finalized menu, Campbell's going on and on about steaming wine glasses, when it all clicks into place.

"What the fuck am I doing?" I say to no one in particular.

"Huh?" Campbell says, confused at my question.

"One of the most important women in my life can't be here, for obvious reason. Steph would have loved this. She would have critiqued the damn thing the entire night, but she would have been flattered to pieces. And since she can't be here, she would be chewing my ear out for not having the woman I love here."

Campbell is still staring at me like I have three heads when I throw the menu down onto the table.

"I have to call an Uber." I jab my fingers into the screen of my phone.

"Uh, what? We're opening in half an hour. This brand new restaurant we're launching is having its opening night in half an hour." My business partner waves his hands in front of my face like I'm having a mental breakdown.

Maybe I am, but I choose to call it a breakthrough. "I have to go get Molly."

"Smith, just wait a minute, calm down—" Campbell is trying to put on that soothing demeanor, and it's not going to work with me.

"No. I'm going to get her," I say, and walk out of the restaurant.

My Uber is minutes away, and I know Campbell might come out here to try and stop me, but he won't succeed. Sometimes, it takes you years to work things out in your head. Whether it's parental issues, competitive streaks, grief, heartbreak ... whatever it may be. And sometimes, it comes into focus all in one nanosecond. As I was staring down at that damn burrata salad, I just *knew*.

All of the bullshit that has been holding me back, the jealousy, insecurities, mourning, fear—it just melted away. I want Molly, and nothing else matters. I'm in love with her, and I've waited too damn long at this point to waste another minute being petty and ridiculous. So yes, sometimes it took a good long while, and sometimes it was simply instinct in one second. Kind of like the way I fell in love with her at first sight.

I'm able to jump into my Uber undeterred, though I'm sure Campbell is calling my siblings for backup to get my ass back to Stefania. It's a torturous twenty-minute ride over to her apartment, and I rifle through every apology there is in my brain as the car zooms through the streets. I have so much to make up to her, and I just pray to God she can hear it and accept it.

I hope like hell that she can love me the way I love her.

I'm pounding on her door, my fist knocking against the flimsy wood, my heart damn near beating out of my chest. A shuffle behind the door, the lock flips, and then she's standing there, drop-dead gorgeous in reading glasses and sweat pants.

"Hi." I breathe reverently, because it's been a while since my eyes drank her in.

"Smith?" Molly looks genuinely confused. "Wait a minute, why are you here? Isn't tonight—"

"I'm sorry. I'm so fucking sorry. Jesus Christ, I've been such a fucking idiot. I should have come here weeks ago. Shit, I should have come to your bedroom that very night." I'm breathing heavy from running up all those flights, from flying over here with adrenaline pumping in my veins.

Her hazel orbs bulge, genuine shock meeting my gaze, and I'm fully aware that I probably look insane right now.

"I don't ... isn't Stefania opening tonight?" Someone must have told her, but I don't know why she thinks that's relevant in the least right now.

I grip the doorjamb, leaning in as much as she'll let me because she hasn't invited me inside. "I didn't lose you to him. I didn't lose you to anyone but my own horrible actions. I'm so fucking sorry, Molly. I lost you because I was a selfish, grief-clouded prick who couldn't see past his own needs to take care of your heart. My brain was all fucked up from your relationship with Justin, from losing my sister, from fearing that I loved you more than you could love me. But none of that matters, it doesn't. It's just bullshit. The one thing that remains is that I love you, and I know you, to your core. You're the best woman, not to mention person, I've ever known. Everything you touch is made better, you make *me* better. And if you can give me one more chance, I promise that I'll show you every single day just how much I cherish you. Just how much I've loved you, just how much I knew you were the other half of me since the first moment I laid eyes on you. I have a lot to prove to you, Molly, but please. Be with me. Love with me. Jesus, fight with me. Fight *for* me. Nothing else matters."

I feel depleted after the last word leaves my lips, but that's all of it. Every truth is laid out between us, and I'm teetering on the edge of a cliff waiting for her answer.

And Molly just starts laughing. Giggling at first, quietly, and then the laughs roll out of her, until tears are streaming down her face.

"Only you. Only you, Smith. Only you could make me want to hit you and kiss you at the same time. You drive me crazy, which is not a natural reaction for me! I'm even-keeled, and you knock me off my axis. How can I want to give into everything you're saying, while I've cursed your name for weeks? It makes no sense!" She just keeps laughing.

"Because you love me," I tell her.

"I should throw you off my doorstep, it's been weeks! I've been crying over you for weeks. And yet, I want to drag you inside." Her eyes become serious, but she's still got that goofy grin.

"Because you love me," I repeat it, hoping that if I'm determined enough in saying it, it will come true.

"You come here, pour your heart out, and just expect me to

take you back without hesitation?" Molly all but stomps her foot.

"No, not without hesitation. But yes, because you love me." I lean in, our noses practically touching.

"And I'll just break down and do it. Because ... I love you." She shrugs, as if she can't help it.

That's all it takes to have me backing her into her apartment and covering her mouth with mine. The kiss is intense, and she throws her arms around my neck, holding tight. I grip her waist, pulling her into me as close as I can. I want to get lost in her, this kiss the first where I know without a doubt that she loves me.

But there is one thing we have to do first. I break off, sucking in a lungful of breath.

"Will you come with me? There is no one else I want to share this night with. Stephanie would have loved you like a sister, she always told me I should just own up to my feelings for you. Please, Mol. Come with me to the restaurant?"

Her smile, tearful and joyful all at the same time, is the same honest expression I fell in love with every day for the last year and a half.

"Of course. That's what you do for the person you love."

39

MOLLY

Smith is lucky I was already showered.

It takes me a hasty twenty minutes to choose an outfit, throw some makeup on my face and make sure my hair doesn't look like a rat's nest. I'm not particularly high maintenance, but for a night like this I would have taken a good hour to primp myself.

This feels more whirlwind though, exactly the way it should feel when you're madly in love in New York City and making decisions on a whim with the man who holds your heart.

When he showed up at my door, the pounding of his fist interrupting my going on three-hour *Hart of Dixie* marathon, I was flabbergasted. It was the last thing I expected, especially since I'd gone out to dinner with Marta just days before and she filled me in on the opening of Stefania. I thought about Smith throughout the night, hoping that he was in a good head space for the launch of the restaurant. It had to be emotional for him, but I knew he wouldn't be going through with it if it wasn't a perfect honor to his late twin.

The words he said to me, the apologies he gave ... they were the ones I've been waiting for. I've been half a person since the night of his birthday, and here he was in front of me, giving me back the thing that lit up the organ in my chest. I don't want to fight that anymore; like Smith said, I want to fight for him. I want to fight for us.

Clearly, we still have a lot of things to talk over. One grand gesture apology does not make up for some very harsh words and weeks of waiting for resolution. There are still lifestyles to mesh together, schedules to work around, and this isn't the summer. We're going to be busier than ever, and it will be a lot of work to maintain a relationship.

But he's the one I want. If I've learned anything in our time apart, it's that Smith wasn't a rebound, or a summer fling. He's the man I was always supposed to be with, the one that it took me a couple wrong turns and some animosity to get to.

Telling him I'm in love with him felt like I was allowing myself to finally be *me*. It wasn't just about matching his feelings, though I'm so glad he now knows that I love him just as much as he loves me, but in doing so, I stepped into who I'm truly meant to be.

As it is, we show up an hour late to his restaurant opening. Smith filled me in on the way over, about how he was staring at the menu, and suddenly his mind cleared. It seems that, for him, things happen all at once. He knew he loved me the minute he saw me. He knew he didn't want to go to college, so he went to work. He wanted to open a restaurant, so he did it. He knew, staring down at that menu, that it was the moment to grovel back to me.

For me, things happened more gradually, but I couldn't deny that I've fallen head over heels for him. We'll figure the rest out later.

Smith has his hand on my back as we walk in, and the restaurant is packed.

"Oh, it's beautiful." I gasp quietly.

I've never been to Italy, but this is what I imagine a posh restaurant in the middle of Rome would look like. There are brick wall accents and cool modern light fixtures. A massive bar covers a whole wall, it's glass bottles shining in the dim mood lighting. The bar top looks like it's made of one whole trunk of a tree, sanded down to be made smooth. There is a massive fireplace raging on the wall across from the bar, and the gold chairs gleam at the sturdy tables dotting the floor.

"I tried really hard with this one. I think Steph would call it adequate." Smith chuckles self-deprecatingly.

"Jesus, there you are!" A tall, brawny man with a buzz cut speed walks over to us.

"Campbell, this is Molly. Molly, my business partner. I fear he may take me off into a corner and chew me out, so excuse his behavior."

Campbell looks on the verge of yelling at Smith no matter who is within earshot, and I'm a little intimated because this guy is no chump. He looks like he could detach that tree trunk from the top of the bar and throw it across the room.

And then someone calls my name, and I see Heather floating across the room. "Mol!"

I'm genuinely confused to see my best friend. "What are you doing here?"

"Marta invited me the other day, and I figured even if I didn't like the dude whose restaurant it is, I'm not saying no to a free martini and passed appetizers."

Smith snorts beside me. "Glad to know that's all it takes to get on your good side."

"My question is, what the hell are you doing here?" Her eyes laser beam down at Smith and my now interlaced fingers.

I shrug. "The guy who owns the restaurant kind of did the hero apology thing."

My best friend is quiet for a moment, and then walks over to pat Smith on the shoulder. "Good job, Mr. Big. Just don't hurt her again, or I'll take a corkscrew to your balls."

"Noted." Smith's blue eyes dance with amusement. "Heather, this is Campbell, my business partner."

Heather finally takes stock of the other man standing in our little huddle, and I know the instant she checks him out. She's interested, I've seen her do this subtle head nod every time she has a man in her line of sight.

"Nice to meet you." Campbell's eyes linger on Heather's body, and I read the sexual chemistry pouring off each of them.

"And you." She flutters her eyelashes.

"Can I interest you in one of our signature cocktails?" he asks, escorting her away with his hand on the small of her back.

"Uh-oh." I chuckle, moving in conspiratorially toward Smith. "What did we just do?"

"Hopefully, a little bit of match-making, if not get each of them laid for at least one night." He grins.

"And I think you just avoided being chewed out."

Smith pulls me into him, nuzzling my ear as our bodies press against each other. "This night is going to be a whirlwind, so I apologize if I can't be with you every second. But before we get sucked into the crowd, I have to tell you, I am so in love with you, Molly."

The smile on my face is so goofy and delirious, I'm kind of happy my expression is buried in his shoulder.

He wasn't lying when he said the opening would be hectic. I went through the first couple of introductions with Smith, but then he started getting into the nitty-gritty professional talk with some of the city's brightest restauranteurs, and I couldn't just stand by and listen.

I found myself talking with his mother, his brothers and sisters, and our summer house friends. They were all surprised, but then again not, to see me at the opening. When his mom hugged me in greeting, she whispered in my ear and said that she knew her son would make things right.

He'd be a fool not to fall in love with a woman like you. That's what she told me.

As my eyes lock with Smith's across the room toward the end of the night, my stomach gives a little flutter. Because I know I get to go home with that man, and we have a lot of making up to do.

40

SMITH

"Do you need my jacket?"

I wrap my arm around Molly's shoulders, and her skin is cool to my touch.

She shakes her head, looking out on the twinkling cityscape. "No, I kind of like the cold. It means winter is coming, and winter in the city is my favorite season."

Funny, it's mine, too. "The bustle of the holidays, the snow on the garbage piles, the sardine crowds in Rockefeller Center."

Molly grins. "Yep, I love it all."

In the background, the notes of a Frank Sinatra song travel through the party, and some people sway on the dance floor under the twinkling lights that serve as a ceiling to the rooftop. One of those couples is Jacinda and Peter, clearly enjoying their own engagement party on the outdoor top floor venue of a beautiful Tribeca hotel. I thought they were a little crazy for doing an outdoor rooftop party in October, but now I kind of get the draw.

Even though the night is cold, they have those industrial heaters set up all around the party. The vibe of it is pure Jacinda, both edgy and relaxed all at the same time. And you can't beat the twinkling lights of the city below, and the view of the bridges out on the Hudson.

"We'll be able to spend Christmas together this year." I pull her farther into me, so that her front is pressed against the railing, and I'm shielding her from the wind at our backs.

"Promise me you'll brave the crowds at the Bryant Park winter village. I love skating on that ice rink." She snuggles back into me.

"Only for you." I chuckle.

It's been a month since we got back together, and our relationship is even better than the summer. Because we talk about our issues, or insecurities that we have being with each other. A lot of those have faded as we've gotten more comfortable, and being in the city helps. There is something about being back in our natural living and working environments that makes our connection and the time we spend with each other feel more real. The beach house, and the way we fell in love, was incredible, but it also felt like we had rose-colored glasses on throughout our stay there. The reason we all went to the Hamptons was to live out a summer fairy tale, to escape the pressure of reality, and so Molly and I ended up doing the same when it came to us.

Now we have to make a concerted effort to spend time together around our work schedules. I have to put up with her nagging me about my lack of cleanliness at her apartment, and she has to listen to me drone on about sports games. I try my best to support her at the end of one of her very long days, where she comes home and cries because one of her students was taken out of an abusive home, or another hasn't shown up to school in a week. Molly shows me that she's the very best of humanity each and every day, and I often feel I don't measure up.

"Maybe we'll have us one of these soon." My tone is sly.

Molly doesn't catch on to what I'm saying. "What, a rooftop? Hate to break it to you, buddy, but I'm not really an Upper East Side kind of girl."

"This is Tribeca, definitely not the Upper East Side. Regardless, I wasn't talking about the area we live in. I'll live wherever you want, as long as it's not New Jersey," I tease her, because I love to tease her about her home state.

"Shush." She digs an elbow gently into my ribs.

"But no, I'm not talking about apartments. I'm talking about an engagement party."

I feel her body go still, and then she flips her head back, blond hair whipping in the cool wind. Her chin is angled up at me, her eyes wide. "Please tell me you're not proposing at someone else's engagement party."

My palm presses to her cheek. "What kind of romantic would I be if I did that? No, I'm not asking you here. But I will be asking you. I just wanted you to know that."

"Smith, we've only been dating for a month." Molly gives a slight shake of her head.

"So? I knew within five seconds of meeting you that you're the woman I want to marry. I love you, and you love me. What else is there to consider?"

"I'm going to be putting up with your split-second decision making my entire life, aren't I?" She smiles.

I nod. "Get used to it, babe."

41

MOLLY

It feels like the cold weather sneaks up on us New Yorkers every year, when in reality, it seeps in between the skyscrapers for months.

And then one day, I'll be walking through the streets, realizing I need to start bringing my gloves out with me everywhere.

As Smith and I speed walk down the street to my apartment, I'm fully aware that those gloves would warm my shivering body right about now. We just went out to dinner at this new ramen place he's been raving about, and not even the two glasses of sake have warmed my blood enough to combat December in the city.

"Your nose is all pink." Smith bends down to kiss it as I fish my keys from my purse.

Letting us through the door to my walk up, I breathe a sigh of relief when the lukewarm air of the tiny lobby hits me. Usually, we stay at Smith's place on the weekends, but the ramen restaurant was closer to my apartment, so here we are. We've worked out a schedule of sorts, my place on school nights, unless he has a really packed night at one of the restaurants, in which case, we sleep separately.

I hate those nights, as does Smith, because they usually come with a horny phone call or a whiny pre-bed FaceTime that I should just let him order me an Uber to go sleep in his bed. He's mentioned once or twice, a hundred times, that we should just move in together, and I admit that he's starting to wear me down.

Smith isn't just my boyfriend, he's my best friend. He's become my shoulder to lean on, the one I want to talk to whenever anything happens, and the person who makes me feel most comfortable.

Once we get upstairs, we unwrap our coats and I jack the heat up on my old radiator.

"Mind if I wash up first?" he asks, an inside joke between us.

We always make reference to our Hampton's days of sharing a bathroom, since it was the place that first cemented our relationship.

"Nope. You go ahead. I'm going to put on some tea." A steaming cup of chamomile is one of my favorite cold night treats.

I hear the water going in the bathroom as I futz around the kitchen, and then head into the bedroom to grab a warm pair of pajamas. We might still be in that honeymoon phase of dating, but I've never been the type of woman to shun clothing, even if it does seem sexier to my sleeping partner. Smith doesn't seem to mind my flannel long johns, in fact, he tells me they're cute.

When he emerges from the bathroom, he has on plaid pajama pants and nothing else. They're hanging so low on his hips that I audibly gulp and consider not putting my own pajamas on just yet if he's going to take them right off.

But I do need to pee, so I head for the bathroom. And there, sitting on the brim of my sink as I walk in, is my boyfriend's toothbrush. I swear to all that is holy …

My annoyance level peaks, thinking back on all the times I asked him to put his shoes by the front door of my apartment, or rinse off a dish before he puts it in my apartment's twenty-year-old dishwasher.

I love the man, but his lack of order and cleanly living has been a sticking point between us. Now I get why Heather gave him so much shit about leaving his cereal bowls in the sink at the Hamptons house.

"Smith, I am going to ..."

I'm about to tell him his toothbrush is going in the garbage, or maybe the toilet if I'm feeling particularly saucy, when I see something sparkle on the handle of it.

"You're going to what?" I hear his deep voice behind me, and when I look back, he's leaning smugly against the doorjamb with his arms folded over his very sexy, very defined pecs.

"What is that?" My throat is suddenly dry, and I'm hesitant to look back at the toothbrush.

Because I'm pretty sure, hanging on the handle of his toothbrush which hasn't been put back in the holder, is a diamond ring.

He told me two months ago at Peter and Jacinda's engagement party that he was going to ask me to marry him. I never thought it would be this soon. Sure, Smith is always saying or doing romantic things, it's one of the things I get to love and have to myself that not many people know about him.

But I thought he was crazy for saying he wanted to propose after we'd only been back together for a month. My heart stutters in my chest, because now I know I'm the crazy one.

Because, for the life of me, I can't think of any reason I should not marry this man. I know he's about to ask, and while it defies all the rules of dating or being an adult, I would go down to city hall right now and make him my husband.

Smith takes hold of my hands, and my fingers are trembling in his.

"You told me a while back that you thought you'd be planning your wedding within the next year. And that stuck with me. Not because you were talking about another man, but because I wanted you to see, so desperately, that I was supposed to be the one you were marrying. I know you might think this is fast, that a lot of people might think that. But I've been in love with you for a long time—what seems like forever—and when I know what I want, I don't wait. I love you, Molly. I promise, I will try for the rest of my life to make you happy, and I'll always keep you safe. Marry me? Make me the happiest damn man on the planet?"

Smith kneels in front of me, reaching around my body to take his toothbrush off the sink and hold it up to me. The diamond ring is cushioned in the grip of the turquoise handle, and I already feel the waterworks pouring down my cheeks.

I'm so glad, so freaking glad that I waited for this moment. That I didn't try to push it with Justin, or go settling for a man that my heart wasn't one hundred percent head over heels for. This is what they mean when they say true love, this right here. Having Smith be the only man to get down on one knee, the only man to ever ask me this question, it makes it all that much more special.

"Yes. Yes! One hundred percent, *yes*." I nod like a maniac, falling into his arms.

He catches me, nearly dropping the toothbrush with the ring hung around it, and I'm showering his face in kisses.

"We're getting married." I sob, so deliriously excited.

Smith pulls back a little, enough so that he can slide the ring onto my left hand. "I can't wait to make you Mrs. Redfield."

As I study the sparkling, gorgeous oval now adorning my ring finger, neither can I.

"Looks like I'll be planning a wedding after all." I burst out laughing.

"The only one you we're ever supposed to plan," Smith confirms, and covers his mouth with mine.

After that, we don't talk for a good, *long* while.

EPILOGUE
MOLLY

One Year Later

How strange it is to be back here, more than a year later, with a ring on my finger and my heart in a completely different place?

Last June, I stepped foot in this beach house with a broken heart, a guarded soul, and the notion that the man rooming right next to me hated my guts. Now, I was watching the sunset from the balcony of my summer house room on the night before my wedding day while the love of my life slept in the room right beside mine. What had started as a summer of self-discovery and reinventing myself had ended with me finding my soul mate.

In those first few weeks in the summer house last year, I lamented that I should have been falling in love with Justin and working toward planning our wedding, our life. And then Smith hit me like a train I couldn't have avoided if I wanted to, and I am sure glad he'd been so upfront. If he hadn't been, I wouldn't be in the place I am now.

Blissfully happy, completely in love, and a nervous wreck.

Because even if I am one hundred and ten percent certain about *who* I am marrying, I have jitters that everything will go as perfectly as I planned it. Heather called me the most precise and organized bride on the planet, and I wouldn't deny that I am. But I am one of those little girls who dreamed of her wedding day, and I want it to go off without a hitch when I get hitched.

We decided not to get married in the summer, since it's way too hot and I've always envisioned a fall wedding. September nuptials might not line up perfectly with my school schedule, but my principal and fellow teachers were helping out while I got to take a honeymoon.

Plus, it's off season in the Hamptons, and that means cheaper stays for our guests and nothing would be as crowded. When Smith had first floated the idea of getting married on the beach just outside our summer rental house, and then holding the reception in the backyard, I balked. My parents were warming up to Smith, thanks to his crazy, loud, blue-collar family they met on several occasions. But it didn't mean they were going to be gung-ho about a Hamptons wedding. Over the course of a couple weeks, though, Smith had plead his case.

It will be a down-to-earth affair, with a dreamy white tent set up on the tennis court, right next to the pool. There are fairy lights and there will be fun music, the sound of the ocean and food from our favorite places we discovered together last summer. All of our closest friends and family are here, and we'll join our lives together while standing on the very beach where Smith first kissed me in front of our roommates. It is perfect, *kismet.*

Smith keeps claiming that he's going to buy this entire beach house, but I keep shushing him and telling him that's a crazy thing to say. Why do I have a feeling, after this, that he's actually going to do it? He'll say that no one else can reside in our beach house, or play on the sand where we got married.

With the success of Stefania, he probably could buy it. Since the restaurant's opening, it's been featured on numerous lists both locally and nationally, and the chef who runs the kitchen won a James Beard award for the food served there. Last month, Smith and Campbell were asked to be guest judges on a very well-known reality cooking show, and they rated so high that the show has asked them on as permanent judges next season.

My fiancé, so weird yet heart-melting to call him that, hasn't decided if he'll take the job yet. It's a lot of intense filming time over twelve weeks, and it's just months after we'll get back from our honeymoon. Smith is wavering, but I think he should do it. We're not the type to hold each other back from something that will make us happy, and I can manage for a few months. I know, deep down, he really wants to do it, and I'll end up nudging him in that direction.

Just like he nudged me to leave my waitress position at Aja, and come work as the front of house manager a couple nights a week at Stefania. Of course, my full-time job is still in teaching. I go to school each day and try my hardest to provide for and support my students. But I'm a natural born worker, I've been raised to have two or even three jobs at a time. I wouldn't, and couldn't ethically, just stop waiting tables because my future husband owned restaurants or made quadruple my annual salary. I told Smith as much, and don't want to rely on his money, though he was firm about combining our accounts. He said that's what married couples do, joined their lives together, and finances were something we were always going to talk about and do together. As logical and mathematical as it is, it was also kind of romantic when he said that.

No, the argument he finally made that convinced me to leave Aja was that I was working for a competing restaurant, and it made sense. Once Smith and I were married, what was his became mine. He's going to be my family, and as such, those restaurants would be my family business. It only made sense for me to come work for him, though he kept saying I didn't need to work a second job at all.

I love it, though. I had so many years of waiting experience, that it was a fun challenge to manage all of the waiters at Stefania and keep the whole floor moving. It also meant I got to spend more time with Smith, because there wasn't a night where he wasn't at one of his three restaurants. Typically, he's at Stefania, and I think it's because he feels closest to his twin sister when he's working there.

Smith honors Steph every day through his work, but he did end up mustering up his courage and giving a speech at her memorial in January. It was beautiful and touching, and cemented even further the idea that he was a kind, caring, giving man. I can't wait to marry him.

From the corner of my eye, I can make out my wedding dress hanging in the closet, and my heart flutters. It's the exact one I've always dreamed of. A strapless A-line lacy beauty that makes me look as elegant as it does makes me look like a princess.

The doorknob to my room jiggles, and then a tiptoeing Smith creeps in, shirtless in nothing but his boxers.

"What are you doing in here? This is bad luck!" I slap my own hands over my eyes, because maybe if I can't see him, he won't see me.

It's dumb logic, but I'm a superstitious bride. I'm also traditional, and told Smith he shouldn't even be sleeping in the bedroom next to me, but he convinced me this was our *thing*. Clearly, it was so he could sneak into my room.

"It's not bad luck at all. Plus, it's almost midnight, which means it's our wedding day. Which means I get to see you as much as I want." I feel his large hands grip my waist, and I can't help but wind my arms around his neck.

My eyes still aren't open though. "Midnight? It's barely nine o'clock, but nice try."

When Smith speaks, his voice tickles my ear, and I feel his lips on the lobe. "Can you blame a man? My soon-to-be wife drives me crazy. How can I keep away when we've done some very scandalous, secret things in these bedrooms?"

My knees practically buckle. *Lord*, does this man know how to literally sweep me off my feet.

Finally, I open my eyes, and Smith's are dazzling before me. "I can't wait to marry you."

"And I can't wait until you're my wife. I think we should practice for the wedding night. *Right now.*"

I throw my head back to chuckle, but Smith is sneaky, taking the opportunity to nibble on my neck. It sends tingles shooting down my spine, and they settle right between my legs.

It seems surreal that tomorrow I'll be walking down the aisle to the man I once thought hated my guts. Now, he's going to be my husband, and I am so ridiculously in love with him that I would probably let him sleep in my room tonight, tradition be damned.

I just couldn't stand to be away from him most times. And tomorrow afternoon, I officially would never have to be again.

Thank you for reading Love at First Fight? In need of another enemies-to-lovers romance to pull at your heart strings? Read When Stars Burn Out now!

ALSO BY CARRIE AARONS

Do you want your **FREE** Carrie Aarons eBook?

All you have to do is sign up for my newsletter, and you'll immediately receive your free book!

Then, check out all of my books, available in Kindle Unlimited!

Standalones:

If Only in My Dreams

Foes & Cons

Love at First Fight

Nerdy Little Secret

That's the Way I Loved You

Fool Me Twice

Hometown Heartless

The Tenth Girl

You're the One I Don't Want

Privileged

Elite

Red Card

Down We'll Come, Baby

As Long As You Hate Me

On Thin Ice

All the Frogs in Manhattan

Save the Date

Melt

When Stars Burn Out

Ghost in His Eyes

Kissed by Reality

The Prospect Street Series:
Then You Saw Me

The Callahan Family Series:

Warning Track

Stealing Home

Check Swing

Control Artist

Tagging Up

The Rogue Academy Series:

The Second Coming

The Lion Heart

The Mighty Anchor

The Nash Brothers Series:

Fleeting

Forgiven

Flutter

Falter

The Flipped Series:

Blind Landing

Grasping Air

The Captive Heart Duet:

Lost

Found

The Over the Fence Series:

Pitching to Win

Hitting to Win

Catching to Win

Box Sets:

The Nash Brothers Box Set

The Complete Captive Heart Duet

The Over the Fence Box Set

ABOUT THE AUTHOR

Author of romance novels such as Fool Me Twice and Love at First Fight, Carrie Aarons writes books that are just as swoon-worthy as they are sarcastic. A former journalist, she prefers the love stories of her imagination, and the athleisure dress code, much better.

When she isn't writing, Carrie is busy binging reality TV, having a love/hate relationship with cardio, and trying not to burn dinner. She lives in the suburbs of New Jersey with her husband, two children and ninety-pound rescue pup.

Please join her readers group, Carrie's Charmers, to get the latest on new books, exclusive excerpts and fun giveaways.

You can also find Carrie at these places:
Website
Amazon
Facebook
Instagram
TikTok
Goodreads